Dear Billy
Happy Birthday

Bryan Cai
May, 2003

TRADITIONAL TALES
OF
Long, Long Ago

This is a Parragon Publishing Book
This edition published in 2001
Parragon Publishing, Queen Street House,
4 Queen Street
Bath BA1 1HE UK

Printed and bound in China
ISBN 0 75254 514 0

Illustrated by
Sue Clarke, Anna Cynthia Leplar, Jacqueline Mair,
Sheila Moxley and Jane Tattersfield

Jacket illustration by Diana Catchpole

TRADITIONAL TALES
OF
Long, Long Ago

p

LITTLE TREASURIES

Retold by
Philip Wilson

Contents

Hudden and Dudden and Donald
    O'Neary   10
Munachar and Manchar   18
Why the Manx Cat Has No Tail   24
The Giant's Causeway   25
The Enchantment of Earl Gerald   32
The Story of the Little Bird   36
A Donegal Fairy   40

The Leprechaun's Gold 41
The Sprightly Tailor 46
Gold-Tree and Silver-Tree 50
Stuck for a Story 56
King O'Toole and his Goose 64
The Frog 70
The Black Bull of Norway 74
The Well at the World's End 82
The Horned Women 86

The Princess of the Blue
    Mountains   92
The Widow's Son and the King's
    Daughter   98
Kate Crackernuts   106
The Son of the King of Ireland   112
The Greek Princess and the
    Young Gardener   120
Canobie Dick   130

The Knight of Riddles   134
The Humble-Bee   140
The Seal Woman   142
Rashen Coatie   146
The Tale of Ivan   152
Cherry of Zennor   158
Skillywidden   168
I Don't Know   170
The Fenoderee   178
A Bride and a Hero   182

The Lazy Beauty	192
Paddy O'Kelly and the Weasel	200
Dream of Owen O'Mulready	208
The King and the Laborer	214
The Legend of Knockgrafton	220
Fair, Brown and Trembling	226
The Haughty Princess	236
The Man Who Never Knew Fear	242
The Missing Kettle	248
Jamie Freel	252

Hudden and Dudden
and Donald O'Neary

Once upon a time there were two farmers, called
Hudden and Dudden. They each had a huge farm,
with lush pastures for their herds of cows, and
hillside fields for their sheep. But no matter how
well they did, they always wanted more.

Between their land was a little field with a tiny
old cottage in the middle, lived in by a poor man
named Donald O'Neary. He only had one cow,
called Daisy, and barely enough grass to feed her.

Although he was only poor, Hudden and Dudden
were jealous of Donald. They wanted to divide his
land between them, to make their farms even
bigger. Whenever the two rich farmers met, they
talked about how they could get rid of poor Donald.

One day, Hudden said, "Let's kill Daisy, then he'll
soon clear out." So, Hudden and Dudden fed some
poison to Daisy, and made off with all speed.

At nightfall, Donald went to Daisy's shed. The cow licked her master's hand affectionately, then collapsed on to the floor, and died.

Donald was saddened at Daisy's death. But he was used to being poor and he began to make a plan. "At least I can get some money for Daisy's hide," he thought. And then he had an idea.

The next day, Donald marched off to the fair in the nearby town, with Daisy's hide slung over his shoulder. Before he got the fair, he stopped in a quiet spot, made some slits in the hide, and put a penny in each of the slits.

11

Then he chose the town's best inn, strode in, hung the hide on a nail, and ordered the best whisky.

The landlord looked at Donald's ragged clothes. "Don't worry," said Donald. "I may look poor, but this hide gives me all the money I want." Donald walked over to the hide, hit it with his stick, and out fell a penny. The landlord was flabbergasted.

"What can I give you for that hide?" he asked. "It's not for sale," replied Donald. "My family have lived off that hide for years." And Donald whacked the hide again, producing another penny.

After the hide had produced more pennies, the landlord could stand it no longer. "I'll give you a whole bag of gold for that hide!" he shouted. Donald gave in, and the deal was struck.

When Donald got home, he visited Hudden. "Would you lend me your scales? I have sold a hide and want to work out what I have made."

Hudden could not believe his eyes as Donald tipped the gold into his scales. "You got all that for one hide?" he asked. He raced round to Dudden's, to tell him what had happened. Dudden could not

believe that Daisy's hide was worth a bag of gold, so Hudden took his neighbor to Donald's hovel. They walked into Donald's cottage, and there was Donald sitting at the table, counting his gold.

"Good evening Hudden; good evening Dudden. You thought you were so clever, with your tricks. But you did me a good turn. Daisy's skin was worth it's weight in gold at the fair."

The next day, Hudden and Dudden killed every single cow and calf in their fine herds. They loaded Hudden's cart and set off to the fair.

When they arrived, Hudden and Dudden each took one of the largest hides, and walked around the market shouting "Fine hides! Who'll buy our fine hides?" Soon a tanner went up to them.

"How much are you charging for your hides?"

"Just their weight in gold."

"You have been in the tavern too long if you think I'll fall for that one," exclaimed the tanner.

Then a cobbler came up to them.

"How much are you charging for your hides?"

"Just their weight in gold."

"What sort of a fool do you take me for?" shouted the cobbler, and landed Hudden a punch in the belly that made him stagger backwards.

14

A crowd soon gathered and one of the crowd was the innkeeper. "What's going on?" he shouted.

"A pair of villains are trying to sell hides for their weight in gold," replied the cobbler.

"Grab them! They're probably friends of the man who cheated me out of a bag of gold yesterday," said the innkeeper. But Hudden and Dudden ran. They got more punches, and some tears in their clothes, but eventually they ran all the way home.

Donald O'Neary saw them coming, and could not resist laughing at them. But Hudden and Dudden were determined to punish Donald. Hudden had grabbed a sack, and Dudden

forced Donald into it and tied it up. "We'll throw him into the Brown Lake!" said Dudden.

But Hudden and Dudden were tired with running from the town and carrying Donald so they stopped for a drink on the way leaving Donald, in his sack, on the inn doorstep.

Once more, Donald thought how he could gain from his problem. He started to shout inside the sack: "I won't have her I tell you!" He repeated this until a farmer, who had just arrived with a drove of cattle, took notice.

"What do you mean?" asked the farmer.

"They are forcing me to marry the king's daughter, but I won't."

The farmer thought it would be fine to marry the king's daughter and never again to get up at dawn to milk the cows.

"I'll swap places with you," said the farmer.

"You can take my herd, and I will get into the sack to be taken to marry the king's daughter."

So the farmer let out Donald O'Neary and got into the sack himself. Donald tied up the cord and drove away the herd of cattle. Hudden and Dudden came out of the inn and picked up their burden. When they reached the lake they threw the sack in, and returned home.

Hudden and Dudden could not believe their eyes when they arrived. There was Donald O'Neary with a large new herd of fine fat cattle.

Donald said, "There's lots of fine cattle down at the bottom of the lake. Why shouldn't I take some for myself? Come along with me and I will show you." When they got to the lake, Donald pointed to the reflections of the clouds in the water. "Don't you see the cattle?" he said. Greedy to own a rich herd like their neighbor, the two farmers dived headfirst into the waters of the lake. And they have never been seen since.

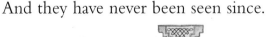

Munachar and Manachar

There were once two little fellows called Munachar and Manachar. They liked to pick raspberries, but Manachar ate them all. Munachar got so fed up with this that he said would look for a rod to hang Manachar.

Munachar found a rod, who asked what Munachar wanted. "A rod, to make a gibbet," he replied.

"You won't get me," said the rod, "unless you get an ax to cut me." So Munachar went to find one. The ax asked what he wanted. "I need an ax, to cut a rod, to make a gibbet," replied Munachar.

"You won't get me," said the ax, "unless you can get a stone to sharpen me." So Munachar went to find a stone. "What do you want?" asked the stone. "I am looking for a stone, to sharpen an ax, to cut a rod, to make a gibbet," replied Munachar.

"You won't get me," said the stone, "unless you can get water to wet me." So Munachar went to find water. "What do you want?" asked the water. "I am looking for water to wet a stone, to sharpen an ax, to cut a rod, to make a gibbet," replied Munachar.

"You won't get me," said the water, "unless you can get a deer who will swim me." So Munachar went to look for a deer. "What do you want?" asked the deer. "I am looking for a deer, to swim some water, to wet a stone, to sharpen an ax, to cut a rod, to make a gibbet," replied Munachar.

"You won't get me," said the deer, "unless you can get a hound who will hunt me." So Munachar went to look for a hound. "What do you want?" asked the hound. "I am looking for a hound, to hunt a deer, to swim some water, to wet a stone, to sharpen an ax, to cut a rod, to make a gibbet," replied Munachar.

"You won't get me," said the hound, "unless you can get some butter to put in my claw." Munachar went to look for butter. "What do you want?" asked the butter. "I am looking for some butter to put in the claw of a hound, to hunt a deer, to swim some water, to wet a stone, to sharpen an ax, to cut a rod, to make a gibbet," replied Munachar.

"You won't get me," said the butter, "unless you can get a cat who can scrape me." So Munachar went to look for a cat. "What do you want?" asked the cat. "I am looking for a cat to scrape some butter, to put in the claw of a hound, to hunt a deer, to swim some water, to wet a stone, to sharpen an ax, to cut a rod, to make a gibbet, " replied Munachar.

"You won't get me," said the cat, "unless you can
get some milk to feed me." So Munachar went to
get some milk. "What do you want?" asked the
milk. "I am looking for some milk to feed a cat, to
scrape some butter, to put in the claw of a hound,
to hunt a deer, to swim some water, to wet a
stone, to sharpen an ax, to cut a rod, to make
a gibbet," replied Munachar.

"You won't get me," said the milk, "unless you
can bring me some straw from those threshers
over there." So Munachar went to ask the threshers.
"What do you want?" asked the threshers. "I am
looking for some straw, to give to the milk, to feed
a cat, to scrape some butter, to put in the claw of a
hound, to hunt a deer, to swim some water, to wet

a stone, to sharpen an ax, to cut a rod, to make a gibbet," replied Munachar.

"You won't get any straw," said the threshers, "unless you bring some flour to bake a cake from the miller next door." So Munachar went to ask the miller. "What do you want?" asked the miller. "I am looking for some flour to bake a cake, to give to the threshers, to get some straw, to give to the milk, to feed a cat, to scrape some butter, to put in the claw of a hound, to hunt a deer, to swim some water, to wet a stone, to sharpen an ax, to cut a rod, to make a gibbet," replied Munachar.

"You'll get no flour," said the miller, "unless you

fill this sieve with water." Some crows flew over crying "Daub! Daub!" So Munachar daubed some clay on the sieve, so it would hold water.

And he took the water to the miller, who gave him the flour; he gave the flour to the threshers, who gave him some straw; he took the straw to the cow, who gave him some milk; he took the milk to the cat, who scraped some butter; he gave the butter to the hound, who hunted the deer; the deer swam the water; the water wet the stone; the stone sharpened the ax; the ax cut the rod; the rod made a gibbet – and when Munachar was ready to hang Manachar, he found that Manachar had BURST.

Why the Manx Cat Has No Tail

In ancient times Noah was collecting together two of every animal to put in his ark. The she-cat would not go in before she had caught a mouse. She thought there might be no mice where she was going, and she was mad for meat.

So while all the other animals were lining up two by two, she was nowhere to be seen.

"Well," said Noah. "There will be no she-cat, and that is all there is to it."

As Noah began to close the door, up ran the she-cat. With a great leap she squeezed through, but the closing door sliced her tail clean off.

No one bothered to mend the tail, so to this day, the cats of Man go tail-less.

But the she-cat thought it was well worth it for the mouse.

The Giant's Causeway

When giants lived in Ireland, there were two who were the strongest and most famous of the giants, Fin M'Coul and Cucullin. Cucullin rampaged all over Ireland, fighting with every giant he met, and always winning. People said that he could make an earthquake by stamping on the ground, and flatten a thunderbolt like a pancake. His strength was said to be in the middle finger of his right hand. Fin was strong too, but he was afraid of Cucullin, and if he heard that the other giant was coming near, Fin found some excuse to move on.

One time Fin and his relatives were building the Giant's Causeway, a great road over the sea to link Ireland and Scotland. Word reached Fin that Cucullin was on his way. "I think I'll be off home for a while to see my wife Oonagh," said Fin. "She misses me when I go away to work."

So Fin set off to his home on top of the hill at

25

Knockmany. Many people wondered why Fin and Oonagh lived there. It was a long climb up but Fin said he chose the place because he liked the view. In truth, he lived there so he could see if Cucullin was coming. And Knockmany was the best lookout for miles around.

As Fin embraced Oonagh, she asked him, "What brought you home so early, Fin?"

"I came home to see you, my love," said Fin, and the couple went in happily to eat.

Oonagh soon realized that he was worried, and guessed there was another reason for his return.

"It's this Cucullin that's troubling me," admitted Fin. "He can make the earth shake by stamping his foot, and flatten a thunderbolt like a pancake. The beast is coming to get me. I don't know what I'm going to do."

"Well, don't despair," said his wife. "I'll help you."

Oonagh called across to her sister Ganua, on the neighboring hill of Cullamore. "Sister, what can you see?" she shouted.

"The greatest giant I ever saw is coming this way. I will call him up my hill and give him refreshment. That may give you and Fin some more time to prepare for him."

Fin was getting even more nervous. All he could think of was the thunderbolt, flattened like a pancake in Cucullin's pocket, and he trembled with fear at what might become of them.

"Your talk of pancakes has given me an idea. I am going to bake some bread," said Oonagh

"What's the point of baking bread at a time like this?" wailed Fin.

But Oonagh ignored him, and started the dough.

She then went out to visit her neighbors, which made Fin even more anxious. She did not seem to be giving a thought to the giant Cucullin.

Oonagh returned with twenty-one iron griddles. She kneaded each one into a portion of the dough, to make twenty-one cakes, each with an iron griddle in the centre. Oonagh baked the bread cakes, put them away and then she sat down to rest, and smiled contentedly.

The next day they spied Cucullin coming up the hill towards their house. "Jump into bed," said Oonagh to Fin. "Pretend to be your own child. Keep quiet, listen to me, and be guided by me."

At two o'clock, Cucullin arrived. "Is this the house of Fin M'Coul?" he asked. "I have heard talk that he says he is the strongest giant in all Ireland, but I want to put him to the test."

"Yes, this is his house, but he is not here. He left suddenly in great anger because someone told him that a great beast of a giant called Cucullin was in the neighborhood, and he set out at once to catch him. I hope he doesn't catch the poor wretch, for

if he does, Fin will knock the stuffing out of him."

"Well I am Cucullin," replied the giant. "I have been searching for him. He will be sorry when I find him – I shall squash him like a pancake."

Fin trembled when he heard the dreaded word "pancake", but Oonagh simply laughed.

"You can't have seen Fin, or you would think differently" she said. But since you are here, could you help me? The wind is blowing at the door making a terrible draught. Turn the house round for me, as Fin would have done if he were here."

29

Cucullin could not believe that Fin had the strength to do this. But he went outside, and turned the building around with his finger, so that the wind no longer blew at the door.

"Now, Fin was telling me that he was going to crack those cliffs on the hill below, to make a spring to bring us water. Will you do that for me, since Fin is not here?" Again, Cucullin was amazed at Fin's strength, and went outside to make a crack in the rocks for the water to come through.

Oonagh thanked him for his help, and offered him some food. With the meat and cabbage, she brought one of the bread cakes she had baked. When Cucullin bit on the bread, he cried out in pain, "Aagh! That's two of my best teeth broken!"

"But that's the only bread that my husband will eat," said Oonagh. "Try another, it may not be so hard." The hungry giant grabbed another, but his hand flew to his mouth in horror:

30

"The Devil take your bread, or I'll have no teeth left!" he roared.

Oonagh pretended to be surprised. "Even our son eats this bread," she said, passing Fin a bread cake with no iron inside.

By now Cucullin was shaking in terror. If the young lad could eat bread like this, what would his father be like? He had to look at the teeth of the child that could eat bread with iron inside.

"It's the back teeth that are the strongest," said Oonagh. "Put your finger into the child's mouth, and feel for yourself."

Fin knew his chance had come. Fin bit hard on the giant's finger, and when Cucullin pulled his hand away in surprise, the middle finger was gone.

Cucullin was crushed. He knew he had lost his strength. He ran from the house, screaming and roaring, and they never saw him again.

The Enchantment of Earl Gerald

Earl Gerald was one of the bravest leaders in Ireland long ago. He lived in a castle at Mullaghmast with his lady and his knights, and if Ireland was attacked, Earl Gerald joined the fight to defend his homeland.

Gerald was also a magician who could change himself into any shape or form that he wanted. This fascinated his wife, but she had never seen Gerald change his shape. Although she had often asked him to show her, Gerald always put her off, until one day her pleading got too much for him.

"Very well," said Earl Gerald. "I will do what you ask. But you must promise not to show any fear. If you are frightened, I will not be able to change myself back again for hundreds of years."

As she had seen him in battle against fearsome enemies, she felt would not be frightened by such a small thing, so Gerald agreed to change his shape.

They were sitting in the castle's great chamber when suddenly Gerald vanished and a beautiful goldfinch flew around the room. His wife was shocked by the sudden change, but stayed calm. She was delighted with the bird, and smiled merrily, when suddenly and without warning, a great hawk swooped through the open windows, diving towards the finch. The lady screamed, even though the hawk missed Gerald and crashed into the table top.

The damage was done. Gerald's wife had shown her fear. As she looked down she realized that the tiny bird had vanished. She never saw either the goldfinch or Earl Gerald again.

Hundreds of years have passed by since Earl Gerald disappeared, and his wife is long dead. Occasionally, Gerald may be seen. Once in seven years, he rides around the Curragh of Kildare. The few who have seen him say that his horse has shoes made of silver, and the story goes that when these shoes are worn away, Gerald will return, fight a great battle, and rule as King of Ireland for forty years.

Meanwhile, in a cavern beneath the old castle of Mullaghmast, Gerald and his knights sleep. They are dressed in full armor and sit around a long table with the Earl at the head. Their horses, saddled and bridled, stand ready. When the right moment comes, a young lad with six fingers on each hand will blow a trumpet to awaken them.

Almost one hundred years ago, Earl Gerald was on a seven-yearly ride when an old horse-dealer passed Gerald's sleeping knights in their cavern. He was amazed to see in the lamp-light the knights in their armor, slumped on the table fast asleep, and the

fine horses waiting there. Suddenly he dropped the bridle he was holding with a clatter and one of the knights stirred in his slumber.

"Has the time come?" groaned the knight. The horse-dealer was struck dumb for a moment, but finally he replied.

"No, not yet. But it soon will."

The knight slumped back on to the table, his helmet giving a heavy clank on the board. The horse-dealer ran away home with all the speed he could manage. And Earl Gerald's knights slept on.

The Story of the Little Bird

Once long ago in Ireland a holy man was walking one day in the garden of his monastery, when he decided to pray to give thanks to God for the beauty of all the flowers, plants and herbs around him. As he did so, he heard a small bird singing the sweetest song he had ever heard. When the bird flew away from the garden, singing as it went, he followed it.

The bird continued its song in a small grove of trees outside the monastery grounds. As the bird hopped from tree to tree, the monk carried on following the little creature, until they had gone a great distance. The more the bird sang, the more the monk was enchanted by the music it made.

The monk realized that it would soon be night-time. Reluctantly, he retraced his steps, arriving back home as the sun was going down in the west. As the sun set, the sky was lit with all the colors of the rainbow, and the monk thought it was almost as beautiful and heavenly as the little bird's song he had been listening to.

But the glorious sunset was not the only sight that surprised the monk. Everything around him seemed changed. Different plants grew in the garden, the brothers had different faces, and even the abbey buildings seemed changed. How could all these changes have taken place in an afternoon?

The holy man walked across the courtyard and greeted the first monk he saw. "Brother, how is it that our abbey has changed so much since this

morning? There are fresh plants in the garden, new faces amongst us, and even the stones of the church seem different."

The second monk looked at him carefully. "Nothing has altered since morning, and we have no new brothers here – except for yourself, for though you wear the habit of our order, I have not seen you before." And the two monks looked at each other in wonder. Neither knew what had happened.

When he saw the brother was puzzled, the holy man started to tell

38

his story, how he had gone to walk in the monastery garden, how he had heard the bird, and how he had followed the creature far into the countryside to listen to its song.

As he spoke the expression on the second monk's face turned from puzzlement to surprise. He said, "There is a story in our order about a brother who went missing after a bird was heard singing. He never returned, and no one knew what befell him, and all this happened two hundred years ago."

The holy man looked at his companion and replied, "That is indeed my story. The time of my death has finally arrived. Praised be the Lord for his mercies to me." The second monk took his confession and gave him absolution, and the holy man died before midnight, and was buried with great solemnity in the abbey church.

Ever since, the monks of the abbey have told this story. They say that the little bird was an angel of the Lord, and that this was God's way of taking the soul of a man who was known for his holiness and his love of the beauties of nature.

A Donegal Fairy

Once an old woman living in Donegal was boiling
a large pot of water over the fire. As the water was
boiling, one of the little people slid down the
chimney and fell with one leg in the hot water.

He screamed a piercing scream, and as the old
lady looked on, dozens of tiny fairies appeared
around the fireplace to pull him out of the water.

"Did the old wife scald you?" asked a tiny figure,
with a menacing tone in his voice.

"No, no, it was my own fault. I scalded myself,"
replied the first fairy.

"Ah, just as well for her," said the rescuer. "If she
had scalded you, we would have made her squeal."

The Leprechaun's Gold

It was Lady Day and everyone who had worked on the harvest had a holiday. Tom Fitzpatrick decided to go for a walk across the fields in the sunshine. After a while he heard a high-pitched noise, "Clickety-click, clickety-click," like the sound of a small bird chirruping.

As Tom peered through some bushes, the noise stopped suddenly, and what did Tom see but a tiny old man, with a leather apron, sitting on a little wooden stool repairing a tiny little shoe the size of his foot. Next to him was a large brown jar.

Tom thought about all the stories he had heard about the fantastic riches of the little people. "I've got it made," he said to himself and he remembered that you should never take your eyes away from one of the little people, otherwise they disappear.

"Good day to you," said Tom. "Would you mind telling me what's in your jar?"

"Beer, the best there is," said the little man.

"And where did you get it from?"

"I made it myself – guess what I made it from."

"I suppose you made it from malt," said Tom.

"Wrong!" said the leprechaun. "It's made from heather!"

"You can't make beer from heather!" said Tom.

" When the Vikings were here in Ireland they told my ancestors how to make beer from heather, and the secret has been in my family ever since. But don't waste time asking me questions. Look – the cows have broken into the corn field and are trampling all over the corn."

Tom started to turn round, but remembered that it was a trick to make him look away from the

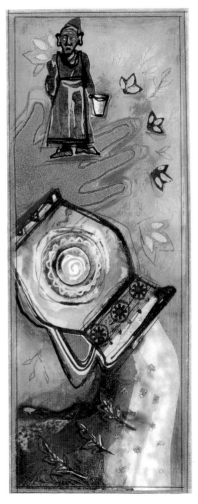

little man. He lunged forward, knocking over the jar of beer, and grasped the little man in his hand.

"That's enough of your tricks!" shouted Tom. "Show me your gold, or I'll squeeze the life out of you before you can blink!"

And Tom made such a fearsome face that the leprechaun began to quake with fright. So he said to Tom, "You just carry me through the next couple of fields, and I'll show you the biggest crock of gold you could imagine."

43

Off they went. No matter how he wriggled and slithered, the little man could not escape Tom's grasp. And Tom looked straight at the tiny creature so that the leprechaun had no chance to disappear.

They walked over fields, across ditches, and through hedges. Finally they arrived at a field that was full of hundreds of turnips. The leprechaun told Tom to walk to the middle of the field, where he pointed towards a large turnip. "You just dig under that one," said the leprechaun, "and you'll find a crock full to the brim with gold coins."

Tom had nothing to dig with and realized that he would have to go home to get his spade. But how would he find the right turnip when he returned? He bent down to remove one of the red ribbons holding up his gaiters, and tied the ribbon around the turnip. "Now you swear to me," he said to the little creature, "that you won't take the ribbon from that turnip before I return."

The leprechaun swore that he would not remove

the ribbon and Tom ran home to get his spade.

When Tom ran back to the turnip field, he was quite breathless. He opened the gate into the field and could not believe his eyes. A mass of red ribbons was blowing in the breeze. The leprechaun had kept his word. He had not taken away Tom's ribbon. Instead he had tied an identical ribbon to every turnip in the field. Tom knew he would never find the gold.

Tom walked sulkily back home, cursing the leprechaun as he went. And every time he passed a turnip field, he gave one of the turnips a mighty wallop with his spade.

The Sprightly Tailor

Long ago, in a castle called Sandell, lived a laird called the great MacDonald. MacDonald's favorite garments were called trews, a combination of vest and trousers in one piece. One day the laird needed some new trews, and called for the local tailor.

When the tailor arrived the great MacDonald told him what he wanted. "I'll pay you extra if you will make the trews in the church by night." He had heard that the church was haunted by a fearful monster, and MacDonald wanted to see how the tailor fared when faced with this beast.

The tailor knew the stories but he liked a challenge – especially if it was going to lead to some extra money. That very night he walked up the glen, through the churchyard, into the dark church.

46

He found a tombstone where he could work, and very soon the trews were taking shape.

After a while, the tailor felt the stone floor begin to shake beneath him. A hole opened up and a large and gruesome head appeared. "Do you see this great head of mine?" a voice boomed.

"I see that, but I'll sew these," replied the tailor, holding up the trews.

Then the head rose higher, revealing a thick, muscular neck. "Do you see this great neck of mine?" the monster asked.

"I see that, but I'll sew these," replied the tailor.

Next the creature's shoulders and trunk came into view. "Do you see this great chest of mine?"

"I see that, but I'll sew these," said the tailor. And he carried on sewing, but to tell the truth some of the stitches were a little less neat than normal.

Now the beast was rising quickly, and the tailor could make out its arms. Its voice echoed in the stone building: "Do you see my great arms?"

"I see those, but I'll sew these," replied the tailor. He gritted his teeth and carried on with his work as before, for he wanted to finish by daybreak and claim his payment from the great MacDonald.

The tailor's needle was flying now. The monster lifted his first leg out of the ground. "Do you see this great leg of mine?" he said, his voice getting even louder.

"I see that, but I'll sew these," replied the tailor. His final stitches were longer, so that he could finish before the monster climbed out of his hole.

As the creature began to raise its other leg, the tailor blew out his candle, gathered up his things, and bundled the trews under one arm. The tailor could hear the creature's footsteps echoing on the stone floor as he ran out into the open air.

Now the tailor could see the glen stretching in front of him, and he ran for his life. The monster roared at him to stop, but the tailor hurried on, and finally the great MacDonald's castle loomed up ahead of him.

Quickly the gates opened and closed behind the tailor – and just as the great wooden gates slammed shut, the monster crashed into the wall.

To this day, the monster's handprint can be seen on the wall of the castle at Sandell. MacDonald paid the tailor for his work, and gave him a handsome bonus for braving the haunted church. The laird liked his new trews, and never realized that some of the stitches were longer and less neat than the others.

Gold-Tree and Silver-Tree

Once there was a king who lived happily with his queen, Silver-Tree, and his beautiful daughter called Gold-Tree. One day Silver-Tree and Gold-Tree were sitting by a pool and it took Silver-Tree's fancy to peer into the water and talk to the trout swimming there: "Silver trout in the pool, who is the most beautiful queen in the world?"

"Gold-Tree is the most beautiful," said the fish.

Silver-Tree was mad with jealousy. She could not stand the fact that someone was more beautiful than she. She decided to get Gold-Tree killed, and to be sure the girl was dead, she would eat Gold-Tree's heart and liver. The queen was so mad with jealousy that she told her husband, begging him to kill their daughter

At just this time it happened that a prince from a far country had come to ask for Gold-Tree's hand in marriage. The king, a good man, seeing that the

two young people loved each other, took his chance and sent the two off to be married. Then, when out hunting, he took a deer's heart and liver, and gave them to his wife. Once she had eaten these, Silver-Tree was cured of her jealousy.

All was well until the queen again asked the fish who was the most beautiful, and he replied "Gold-Tree your daughter is the fairest."

"My daughter is long dead!" exclaimed the queen.

"Surely she is not. For she has married a fine

51

prince in a far country."

Her husband told her that this was true.

"Make ready the great ship, for I must visit my daughter," said Silver-Tree. And because she had seemed cured of her jealousy, the king let her go.

The prince was out hunting when Silver-Tree arrived. Gold-Tree realized that her life was in danger, so she called her servants who locked her in her room. But Silver-Tree was cunning. She called sweetly, "Put your little finger through the keyhole, so your mother may kiss it."

As soon as it appeared, the wicked queen took a dagger dipped in poison and stuck it into Gold-Tree's finger. Straight away, the princess collapsed, and died, the dagger still in her finger as she lay.

When Gold-Tree's husband returned, he was horrified to see his young wife dead on the floor. She was so beautiful that he preserved her body locked in her room, and kept the key himself.

Some years later, the prince's grief faded a little, although he never smiled, and he decided to marry once again. He did not tell his second wife about Gold-Tree's body, but one day she found the key to the dead girl's room. She was curious to see an unknown part of her husband's castle, so she quietly opened the door and went in. When she saw the beautiful body she realized at once that this must be Gold-Tree, for she had heard the tale of the girl's death. She saw the poisoned dagger still stuck in the girl's finger. Yes, this must be Gold-Tree. Still curious, the second wife pulled at the dagger to remove it, and Gold-Tree rose, alive, just as was before her mother's visit.

The second wife said to the prince, "What would you give me if I made you laugh again?"

"Nothing could make me laugh, unless Gold-Tree was alive again," said the prince sadly.

The wife took the prince to the room and he saw Gold-Tree was alive. A change came over her husband and the second wife knew that Gold-Tree was his true love.

"Now you have your true love back," she said, "I must go away."

But the prince was so grateful to her that he would not let her go.

Everything went well for them living together in the palace until Silver-Tree talked to the fish again and discovered that Gold-Tree was still alive and was still the most beautiful woman in the world.

And so Silver-Tree went once more to visit her daughter, and again the prince was out when she arrived. Gold-Tree quaked with fear when she saw her mother approaching. "Let us go to meet her," said the second wife calmly, and they went as if to greet a welcome guest.

Silver-Tree held out a precious gold cup. "I bring a refreshing drink for my daughter," she said.

The second wife looked at her coldly. "It is our custom for the visitor to drink first," she said.

Silver-Tree raised the cup to her mouth, but she knew that if she drank, she would kill herself. Just at that moment, the second wife struck the cup, sending some of the deadly poison straight down Silver-Tree's throat. The wicked queen fell dead to the floor, and the servants took her body to bury her. At last, Gold-Tree, the prince, and his second wife could live in peace.

55

Stuck for a Story

There was once a king of Leinster whose pastime was listening to stories. Before the king went to sleep he called his best storyteller to him, who told him a different story each night. Whatever problems had troubled the king during the day were eased away by the storyteller, and the king always had a good night's sleep. In return, the king granted his storyteller a big house and acres of land, for he thought that the storyteller was one of the most important men in his entire kingdom.

Each morning the storyteller went for a walk around his estate to think up his next story. But one morning, he could not think of a new tale. He seemed to be unable to get beyond "There was once a king of Ireland" or "In olden times there was a great king with three sons".

His wife called the storyteller in to breakfast, but

he said he would not come in until he had a story.
Then he saw an old, lame beggarman in the
distance, and went up to talk to him.

"Good morning to you. Who might you be, and
what are you doing here?" asked the storyteller.

"Never mind who I am," replied the old man.
"I was resting, for my leg is painful. Would you
play a game of dice with me?"

The storyteller thought the old man would have
little money to gamble with, but the beggar said
he had a hundred gold pieces, and the storyteller's
wife said, "Why don't you play with him?
A story might come to you afterwards."
And so the two men began
to throw.

Things did not go well for the storyteller. Soon he lost all his money, but the old man still asked him to play another game. "I have no money left," said the storyteller.

"Then play for your chariot, horses and hounds," said the old man. The storyteller was unwilling to take the risk, but his wife encouraged him.

So they threw the dice, and again the storyteller lost the game.

"Will you play again," said the old man.

"Don't make fun of me," said the storyteller. "I have nothing to stake."

"Then play for your wife," said the beggar. Once again, the storyteller was unwilling, but again his wife encouraged him, so they played and the storyteller lost once more.

The storyteller's wife went to join the beggar.

"Have you anything else to stake?" asked the old man. The storyteller remained silent, so the old man said simply, "Stake yourself."

Again the storyteller was the loser. "What will you do with me?" asked the storyteller.

"What kind of animal would you prefer to be, a fox, a deer, or a hare?"

The storyteller decided that he would rather be a hare, so he would be able to run away from danger. The old man took out a wand and turned the storyteller into a hare. Then his wife called her hounds, and they chased the hare round the field, and all along the high stone wall around it. And all the while the beggar and the storyteller's wife laughed to see the hare twist and turn to try to avoid the hounds. The hare tried to hide behind the wife but

she kicked him back into the field. When the hounds were about to catch him the beggar waved his wand and the storyteller reappeared in the hare's place.

The beggar asked the storyteller how he liked the hunt, the storyteller said he wished he was a hundred miles away. The beggar waved his wand, and the storyteller found himself in the castle of the lord Hugh O'Donnell. What was more, the storyteller realized quickly that he was invisible.

Soon the beggar arrived at O'Donnell's castle.

"Where have you come from and what do you do?" asked the lord.

"I am a traveler and magician," said the beggar and then began playing tricks on O'Donnell's men. "Give me six pieces of silver to show you that I can move one of my ears without the other."

"Done," said one of O'Donnell's men. "You'll never do that, even great ears like yours!"

The beggarman then put one hand to one of his ears, and gave it a sharp pull.

O'Donnell roared with laughter, and paid the

beggar six pieces of silver, but his man wasn't pleased.

"Any fool could do that." he said. Then the man gave his own ear a mighty pull – and off came ear and head together.

Everyone in the castle was dumbstruck. The beggar said "This is an even better trick." He took out a ball of silk and threw it up into the air, where it turned into a thick rope. Then he sent a hare racing up the rope, followed by a hound to chase it.

"Who will catch the hound and stop it eating my hare?" challenged the beggar. Sure enough, one of O'Donnell's men ran up the rope, and everyone below waited. When nothing had happened for a

while the beggar began to wind up the rope, and sure enough, there was the man fast asleep and the hound eating the hare. The old beggar was angry that the man had failed, so he drew his sword, and beheaded both man and hound.

O'Donnell was enraged. The beggar said "Give me ten pieces of silver for each of them, and they shall be cured."

O'Donnell paid over the silver, and the men and hound were restored to their former health. The beggar vanished, taking the invisible storyteller with him.

The storyteller found himself back at the court of the King of Leinster, with the beggar beside him. The king was looking for his storyteller, but instead there was the old beggar, who started to insult the royal harpers. "Their noise is worse than a cat purring over its food," said the beggar.

"Hang this man," shouted the king.

But the beggar escaped, and they found that the king's favorite brother was mysteriously hanged in his place.

"Get out!" roared the king.

But before he went, the beggar made the storyteller visible again, and gave him back his chariot, his horses, his hounds – and his wife. "I had heard you were in difficulties," he said to the storyteller. "Now you have the stories to tell the king." Sure enough, the king thought the new story was the best he had ever heard. From then on, it was the tale the king always wanted to hear, and the storyteller never had to think up a new story again.

King O'Toole and his Goose

Many years ago lived a king called O'Toole. He was a great king who loved to ride all over his realm, through the woods and the fields, hunting deer.

But as time went by the king grew old, and he could no longer ride and hunt. He became sad and bored, and did not know what to do. Then one day he saw a flock of geese flying overhead. O'Toole admired the birds' graceful flight, and decided that he would buy a goose to amuse himself. The king loved to watch the goose flying around, and every Friday, the bird dived into the lake and caught a trout for O'Toole to eat.

The graceful flight of the goose, and the tasty fish she caught, made O'Toole happy. But the goose grew old like her master, and couldn't amuse the king or catch fish for him. O'Toole became sad, again and thought of drowning himself in his lake.

O'Toole was out walking and he saw a young man he had not met before.

"God save you, King O'Toole," said the young man.

"Good day to you," said the king. "How did you know my name?"

"Oh, never mind," said Saint Kavin, for it was he. "I know more than that. How is your goose today?"

"But however did you know about my goose?" asked the king.

"Oh, I must have heard about it somewhere."

King O'Toole was fascinated that a total stranger should know so much about him, so he started to

talk with the young man. Eventually, O'Toole asked Kavin what he did for a living.

"I make old things as good as new, said Kavin."

"So you're some sort of magician?" asked O'Toole.

"No, my trade is better than that. What would you think if I made your old goose as good as new?"

At this, the king's eyes nearly popped out of his head. It seemed impossible that the crippled creature could be restored to health.

Kavin looked at the goose. "I don't work for nothing. What will you give me if she flies again?"

The king looked around him, thinking of his great kingdom, and looked at the poor old goose. He wanted nothing more than to see this bird healthy once more. Even his kingdom seemed paltry by comparison. "I will give you anything that you ask for," replied King O'Toole.

"That's the way to do business

Will you give me all the land
that the goose flies over on
her first flight?"

"I will," said the king.

"Then it's a bargain," said
Saint Kavin.

With that the saint
beckoned to the goose.
Saint Kavin picked her up
by her wings, and made the
sign of the cross on her back.
He threw her into the air, saying "Whoosh!"
The goose soared up into the air, and was flying,
high and fast, just as she used to.

King O'Toole could not believe his eyes. He stared
up into the sky, with his mouth open in amazement,
his eyes following every beat of the goose's wings
and every turn of her flight. She seemed to be
flying further, and higher, and more gracefully than
ever before. Then the goose made a final turn and
swooped down, to land at the king's feet, where he
patted her gently on the head.

"And what do you say to me," said Saint Kavin, "for making her fly again?"

"It goes to show that nothing beats the art of man, and that I am beholden to you." said O'Toole.

"But remember your promise," went on Kavin. "Will you give me every patch of ground, every field and every forest, that she has flown over on her first flight?"

King O'Toole looked at the young man. "I will," he said. "Even though she has flown over every acre of my kingdom. Even if I lose all my lands."

And then the king showed the young man all the lands of which he was now master. Finally Saint Kavin made himself known at last to King O'Toole. "I am Saint Kavin in disguise. I have done all this to test you. And you have done well, King O'Toole. I will give you food, drink, and somewhere to live now that you have given up your kingdom."

"Do you mean all this time I have been talking to the greatest of the saints, while I just took you for a young lad?" said the flabbergasted O'Toole.

"You know the difference now," replied Kavin.

Kavin was good as his word, and looked after O'Toole in his old age. But neither the king nor the goose lived long. The goose was killed by an eel when she was diving for trout, and the old king perished soon afterwards. The king refused to eat his dead goose, for he said that he would not eat what Saint Kavin had touched with his holy hands.

The Frog

A widow was baking in her kitchen and asked her daughter to go down to the well to fetch some water. When the daughter arrived at the well by the meadow, she found that it was dry. This made her wonder what she and her mother would do without water as there had been no rain for days and the poor girl sat down and began to cry.

Suddenly, through her sobbing, the girl heard a noise, and a frog jumped out of the well.

"What are you crying for?" asked the frog.

The girl explained that there was no water and she did not know what to do.

"Well," said the frog, "if you will be my wife, you shall have all the water you need."

The girl thought that this was all a joke, and agreed to be the frog's wife. She lowered her bucket into the well again, and sure enough, when she pulled it up, the bucket was full of water.

The girl went back to her mother and thought no more about the frog until it was evening. Then as the girl and her mother were going to bed, they heard a small voice at the door of their cottage: "Open the door, my own true love. Remember the promise you made to me down at the well."

"Ugh, it's a filthy frog," said the girl.

"Open the door to the poor creature," said her mother, for she liked to be kind to all animals. And so they opened the door.

"Give me my supper, my own true love. As you promised me when you fetched your water down at the well," the frog went on.

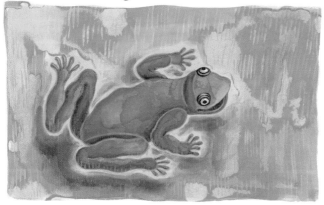

"Ugh, I don't want to feed the filthy beast," said the daughter.

Her mother insisted, and the frog ate all the food thankfully, then he said "Put me to bed, my own true love. As you promised me when you fetched your water down at the well."

"Ugh, I can't have that slimy thing in my bed," protested the daughter.

"Put the poor creature to bed and let it rest," said the mother. So they turned down the sheets and the frog climbed into bed.

Then the frog asked: "Bring me an ax, my own true love. As you promised me when you fetched your water down at the well."

This puzzled the widow and her daughter. "What does the creature want with an ax?" asked the girl. "It is far too heavy for a frog to lift."

"Fetch him an ax," said the mother. "We shall

72

soon see." So the daughter went out to the woodshed and returned with the ax.

"Now chop off my head, my own true love. As you promised when you fetched water down at the well," croaked the frog.

Trembling, the girl turned to the frog. She raised the ax, just as she did when chopping wood for the fire, and brought it down on to the frog's neck. When she had done the deed, the girl looked away for a moment, scared to see the dead creature and its severed head. But when she heard her mother's shout of surprise she looked back quickly. And there stood the finest, most handsome young prince that either of them had ever seen.

"You promised to marry me," smiled the prince.

And the poor widow's daughter and the handsome prince *did* marry, and they lived in happiness for rest of their lives.

The Black Bull of Norway

Long ago in Norway there lived a woman who had three daughters. One day the eldest daughter told her mother that she had decided to seek her fortune. She went to see the witch-washerwoman who could foretell people's futures. The old witch-washerwoman said to her, "Stand by my back door and see what you can see."

The first day, the girl could see nothing unusual, and nothing came on the second day. But on the third day, a fine coach pulled by six horses appeared.

The girl told the witch-washerwoman what she had seen. "That's for you," she said to the girl, who got into the coach and rode away.

Soon the second daughter decided she too should seek her fortune, and also went to the witch-washerwoman's house. The first day, the girl could see nothing unusual, and nothing came on the second day. But on the third day, a fine coach appeared. "That coach is for you," said the witch-washerwoman, and the second daughter rode off.

Then the youngest daughter also decided to visit the witch-washerwoman, who said "Stand by my back door and see what you can see."

75

She could see nothing on the first day or the second day. But on the third day, a great black bull appeared, bellowing as it walked. "That's for you," said the witch-washerwoman.

The girl was fearful of the creature, but climbed on to the beast's back, and they galloped away together. The bull was kind, and when the girl felt hungry and asked for food, the bull said, "Eat from my right ear, and take drink from my left."
The girl did so, and felt wonderfully refreshed.

By and by the bull slowed down at the gate of a fine castle. "Here lives my eldest brother," said the bull, and the two rested for the night at the castle. In the morning, the lord of the castle gave the girl an apple and said, "Do not break into this apple until you are in great need. Then it will help you."

They rode on for many miles, until they arrived at a second castle, bigger and fairer than the first. "Here lives my second brother," said the bull, and the two rested there for the night.

In the morning, the lord of the castle gave the girl a pear. And he spoke to her rather as the first

lord had done. "Do not break into this pear until you are in great need. Then it will help you."

Again the two traveled on, until they came to a third castle, even finer than the others. "Here lives my youngest brother," said the bull, and the lord of the castle gave them lodgings for the night.

In the morning, the lord of the castle gave the girl a plum. "Do not break into this fruit until you are in great need. Then it will help you."

Off they went again, and after another long ride,

the bull came to a halt in a dark and lonely glen. "You must get down," the bull said. "For the time has come when I must go to fight the devil. Sit down on that stone and do not move from here, for if you move I shall not find you. Look around you, and if everything turns blue, I shall have won; but if all turns red that will mean I have lost."

After a while everything in the glen turned blue, and the girl's heart was filled with joy. She was so pleased that she moved one foot and crossed it over the other, quite forgetting her instruction to stay absolutely still. So no matter how long she sat the bull could not find her again.

When the black bull did not return, the girl saw why and knew that she must complete her journey alone. Off she went until she came to a great hill made of glass. She walked around it, but could not climb the glassy surface of the hill. She found a smith, who made her some metal shoes so that she could cross the hill in safety.

The girl climbed the glassy hill, and made her way carefully down the other side, and what

78

should she see but the
house of the old witch–
washerwoman – she had
traveled full circle.
The washerwoman and
her daughter told her of
a handsome knight who
had brought blood-stained
shirts to be washed. He
had promised to marry the
woman who could wash
away the stains, but neither
of them could do this.

The girl washed the shirts,
and both the other women
were envious when they
saw the stains disappearing.
But when the knight
returned for his shirts, the
washerwoman told him
that it was her daughter
who had washed them.

And so it happened that the knight and the washerwoman's daughter prepared to get married.

The girl wondered what to do, since she wanted the truth to be known. She decided to open the apple from the first castle and found a heap of gold and jewels. "Delay your marriage for one day," she said to the daughter, "and these jewels are yours."

The bride-to-be agreed, and the girl planned to explain all to the knight. But the washerwoman realized and gave the knight a sleeping-potion. Through her tears, the girl sang a snatch of song:

The bloody shirt I washed for thee.
Will you not waken and turn to me?

Next day, the girl broke open her pear. Out came jewels even more precious than those that had come out of the apple. "Delay your marriage for one day," said the girl to the daughter, "and you shall have them all."

The washerwoman's daughter agreed, and the girl was ready

to go to the knight. But again the washerwoman gave him a sleeping-potion. And again the girl sang through her tears of sadness:

The bloody shirt I washed for thee.
Will you not waken and turn to me?

The next day one of the knight's men said to him, "What was that singing and moaning last night outside your chamber?" The knight decided that nothing should make him sleep the next night.

Meanwhile, the girl opened the plum and still richer jewels fell out. She offered them to the daughter, who again accepted them. But this time, the knight only pretended to drink the potion.

And so the knight came to hear the truth. The girl who had ridden the black bull, climbed the glass hill, and washed the blood-stained shirt finally married her knight. And the washer-woman's daughter was content with her jewels.

The Well at the World's End

There was once a king, a widower, with a daughter who was beautiful and good-natured. The king married a queen, a widow who had a daughter who was as ugly and ill-natured as the king's daughter was fair and good. The queen loathed the king's daughter, no one noticed her own girl while this paragon was around, so she made a plan. She sent the king's daughter to the well at the world's end, with a bottle to get some water, thinking she would never come back.

The girl had walked far and was tired when she came upon a pony. The pony looked at the girl and spoke: "Ride me, ride me, fair princess."

"I will ride you," said the girl, and the pony took her over a moor covered with gorse and brambles.

Far she rode, and finally she came to the well at the world's end. But the well was too deep and she could not fill the bottle. Three old men came up to her, saying, "Wash us, wash us, fair maid."

She washed the men and in return they filled her bottle with water from the well, then the three men looked at the girl, "She will be ten times more beautiful," said the first. "A diamond, a ruby and a pearl shall drop from her mouth whenever she speaks," predicted the second. "Gold and silver shall appear when she combs her hair," said the third.

The king's daughter returned to court, and to everyone's amazement, the predictions came true.

All were happy, except for the queen and her daughter. The queen decided that she would send her daughter to the well at the world's end, to get her the same gifts. After traveling, the girl came to the same pony, but when the creature asked her to ride it, the queen's daughter replied, "Don't you see I am a queen's daughter? I will not ride you, you filthy beast."

The proud girl soon came to the moor covered with gorse and brambles. It was hard going for the girl, and the thorns cut her feet badly.

After a long and painful walk across the moor, she came to the well at the world's end. Lowering her bottle, she too found that it would not reach the water in the well. Then she heard the three old men speaking: "Wash us, wash us, fair maid."

And the proud daughter replied,

"You nasty, filthy creatures, do you think a queen's daughter can be bothered to wash you?"

The old men refused to dip the girl's bottle into the well. They predicted her future: "She will be ten times uglier," said the first. "When she speaks, a frog and a toad will jump from her mouth," said the second. "When she combs her hair, lice and fleas will appear," said the third.

With these curses ringing in her ears, the unhappy girl returned home. Her mother was distraught, for her daughter was uglier than before, and covered in frogs, toads, fleas, and lice. In the end, she left the king's court, and married a poor cobbler. The king's fair and good-natured daughter married a handsome prince, and was happy – and good-natured – for the rest of her long life.

The Horned Women

Five hundred years ago all well-to-do women had
to learn how to prepare and card their wool and
spin it to make yarn. One evening, a rich lady sat
up late in her chamber, carding a new batch of
wool. Everyone else was in bed; the house was quiet.
Suddenly, there was loud knocking at the door and
a high-pitched voice shouted "Open the door!"

The lady of the house, who did not recognize the
voice, was puzzled. "Who is it?" she called.

"I am the Witch of One Horn," came the reply.

The lady could not hear clearly and thought it was
a neighbor needing help, so she rushed to the door
and threw it open. She was astonished to see a tall
woman, with a single horn growing in the middle
of her head. The newcomer who was carrying a
pair of carders, strode across the room, sat down,
and set to work carding some of the lady's wool.

She worked in silence, then suddenly she said, "Where are all the others? They should be here."

Straight away, there was another knock on the door. Although she was rather frightened, the lady of the house opened the door. To her surprise another witch came into the room, this time with a pair of horns and carrying a spinning wheel.

"Make room for me," she said. "I am the Witch of Two Horns." And no sooner had she said this than she started to spin, producing fine woollen yarn faster than anyone the lady had seen before.

Again and again there came knocks on the door, and the lady felt she had to let in all the newcomers until there were twelve, each with one horn more than the previous witch. They all sat around the fire, carding and spinning and weaving. The lady of the house wanted to run away, but her legs would not let her; she wanted to scream, but her mouth would not open. She realized that she was under the spell of the horned women.

As she sat watching them, wondering what she could do, one of the witches called to her: " Bake us all a cake."

The lady found she could stand up but she couldn't find a pot to collect water from the well. One of the hags said to her, "Here, take this sieve and collect some water in that."

The lady knew that a sieve could not hold water, and as the water poured through the sieve, the lady sat down and cried. Then she heard a voice, that seemed like the spirit of the well. "There is some clay and moss nearby. Mix them together to make a lining for the sieve."

The lady did as she was told, and the voice spoke again. "Go back and scream three times and shout as loudly as you can: 'The mountain of the Fenian women is all aflame.'"

As soon as the lady screamed she was echoed by the cries of the horned women. They all flew off to their mountain, Slievenamon, and the lady was released from the spell. She sighed a huge sigh of relief, but she saw quickly that the witches had made their own cake and poisoned the rest of her family.

The lady turned to the well, asking the spirit "How can I help everyone? And what if the witches return?"

So the spirit told the lady what to do. She had to sprinkle on her threshold water in which she had washed her child's feet. Next she was to put a piece of the witch's cake in everyone's mouth, to bring them back to life. Then the spirit told her to put the cloth woven by the witches into her chest. And finally she was to place a heavy oak beam across the door. The lady did all these things, and waited.

Soon the twelve witches returned, screaming and howling, for they had arrived at their mountain and found no fire, and were mad for vengeance.

"Open the door! Open, foot-water!" they yelled.

"I cannot open," called the water, "I am scattered all over the ground."

"Open the door! Open wood and beam!" they shouted, their noise could be heard over the hills.

"I cannot open," said the door. "For I am fastened with a stout crossbeam."

"Open the door! Open cake that we made with

our enemies' blood!" they screamed – they could be heard by the sea.

"I cannot open," said the cake. "For I am broken in pieces."

Then the witches knew they were defeated, and returned to their mountain, cursing the spirit of the well.

When the lady of the house went outside, she found a cloak that one of the witches had dropped. She hung the cloak up in her room, and it was kept in her family for five hundred years, in memory of her victory over the twelve horned women.

The Princess of the Blue Mountains

There was a poor widow with one son called Will. He was all she had in the world so he always had his way, and he became lazy. In the end she said to him, "Son, you must make your own way in the world. Then you will know what it is to find your own work and earn your own living." So young Will went off to seek his fortune.

Will traveled until he came to a river, which he had to cross. Seeing the rapid current and the sharp rocks he was afraid to go into the water, but a lady on the opposite bank saw him and waved at him to cross, which finally he did.

When Will got to the other side, the lady said she would give him food and drink if he would go into her garden and find the most beautiful flower. But Will, struck by the lady's beauty, said "You are the fairest flower in all the garden."

Charmed by Will, the lady turned to him. "Would you be my husband?" she asked. "There will be many dangers, but I will help you." It did not take Will long to say "Yes, I will be your husband, whatever dangers I must face."

The lady explained her story. She was the Princess of the Kingdom of the Blue Mountains. She had been stolen by a demon called Grimaldin who would do battle with Will. The lady gave Will three black sticks, one for each legion of demons, and a pot of ointment, in case he should be injured. "Use these things well, for now I must leave you."

The lady left and three legions of demons appeared. They beat Will with fearsome clubs, but the young man stopped their blows, and used the lady's sticks to beat them. Soon they were gone.

The lady returned, and was pleased to see Will hale and hearty. "Never has any man fought off the demons with such skill and courage. Tonight, twice as many demons will challenge you, so I will give you six sticks." And the lady left, giving Will a larger pot of ointment, in case he was wounded.

Sure enough, six legions of demons arrived to do battle with Will and he beat them off successfully.

The following morning the lady was delighted but said "I must give you twelve sticks, for twelve legions will come tonight. Look out for Grimaldin, for he will come too." She left more ointment, for no one had survived a fight with Grimaldin without being sorely wounded.

Grimaldin and his twelve legions arrived, and the chief demon asked Will: "What is your business?"

"To rescue the Princess of the Blue Mountains."

"Then you shall die."

The demons attacked, and Will beat them off
with the sticks, but this time Grimaldin attacked,
and struck Will to the ground. The young man
quickly applied the ointment and was amazed to
feel well again. This time, he beat off the chief
demon, who went away, howling.

The princess reappeared looking relieved. "Your
greatest danger is over," she said to Will. "Take this
book about the history of my family; let no one
distract you from reading it. If you know all that is
in this book, you will be one of my father's
favorites, and he will allow you to marry me."

Will started the book. Voices tried to distract him, but he kept his eyes glued to the pages. He heard a woman selling apples and he looked up from the book. He was thrown against the apple woman's basket with such force that he passed out.

When Will awoke there was an old man sitting nearby and Will asked if he knew how to get to the kingdom of the Blue Mountains. The man did not know, so he asked the fishes, and no fish knew the whereabouts of the kingdom. The old man said "I have a brother, who can talk to the birds of the air.

96

He will know, or will find out from the birds."

The old man's aged brother called all the birds but none knew until the last bird, a great eagle, arrived. "I can take you to the kingdom," said the eagle, "Climb onto my back."

They landed by a house hung with black drapes. The people told Will that their master was to be fed to a giant who ate a human victim every day. Whoever could kill the giant would please the king, and gain the hand of his daughter in marriage.

Will knew what he must do. He put on his armor, and strode out to challenge the giant. They fought long and hard, and Will was finally the winner. The princess recognized him and when the king learned that he had killed the giant, gave his permission for Will and the princess to marry. After the wedding, Will's mother came to live with them at the royal castle, and they were all happy together.

The Widow's Son and the King's Daughter

The father of a young lad called Jack died, leaving Jack and his mother penniless so Jack had to go to work. He knew that he was no use at home, so he set off one day to seek his fortune.

After traveling far on the first day, Jack came to a house near a wood. The people of the house offered him food and a bed for the night and the man of the house asked Jack if he needed work. Jack replied that he did. "I have a herd of cattle that needs minding," said the man. "But do not go into the field with the fruit trees. A giant lives in that field and he will surely gobble you up if you go there. He may even carry off my cattle to eat."

Jack went to the field to mind the cattle, and he had not been there long when he started to admire the fruit on the trees in the neighboring field. There were red apples and ripe pears, as well as other fruit that Jack did not know. No one seemed to be about, so Jack thought he would risk a dash into the giant's field for some fruit.

As Jack picked some of the fruit, an old woman passed along the lane by the edge of the field. She was admiring the fruit, and asked Jack to pick some for her. Looking around him to make sure the giant was not coming, Jack agreed, and soon they both had some fine, succulent fruit to eat.

"I will give you something useful in return for your favor," the old woman said to Jack. "Here are three stout rods and a sword. Whoever you stab

with this sword, they will fall down dead. You need never fear your enemies."

Jack thanked the old woman, for he had been worried about the giant, and wondered whether it would stride over the hedge into his field and take his revenge for the stolen fruit.

It was not long before the giant appeared and Jack hastily climbed a tree. He had not tried the sword and wondered whether it would work. This did not put off the giant, who stepped towards the tree, held out his hand, and heaved. He tore the tree up by the roots, and as Jack fell to the ground, Jack's sword grazed his flesh. The giant fell down dead.

Jack was guarding his master's cattle the next day, when another giant appeared. "You dare to slay my brother?" the beast bellowed. Jack drew his sword and felled the beast with one blow. As he looked at the massive corpse, Jack wondered if there were any more in the giant's family.

On the third day, another giant appeared. Jack hid in the hollow of a tree, and heard the creature saying he must eat one of Jack's beasts. "Ask me first," shouted Jack from inside the hollow tree.

"Is it you, who killed my two brothers?" roared the giant. "I shall take my revenge." But as the giant drew near the tree, Jack leaped out and stabbed him. The last of the giants was dead.

When he had got his breath back, Jack decided to go to the giants' castle to see what riches might be hidden there. When he arrived, he told the giant's steward that he had conquered the giants, and, amazed at Jack's strength, he gave the lad the keys to the castle treasuries. Jack took some of the money then traveled back home.

Jack's country was in turmoil when he arrived. People told him that a fire-breathing monster had arrived and had demanded one young boy or girl to eat every day. Tomorrow, it was the turn of the king's daughter.

Jack put on his armor, took his faithful sword and went to see the king's daughter. He told her that he had come to save her, and asked if she would marry him if he was successful. She agreed, and Jack fell at her feet. He was soon asleep with his head in the princess's lap and the princess wove a good-luck charm of white stones in his hair.

Suddenly, the monster crashed into the room. Jack woke up and in one movement he jumped up and drew his sword. He aimed many blows at the monster, but he could not wound the beast because of the fire that came spurting from the creature's mouth. They carried on like this for some time, Jack waving his sword and the beast spitting fire,

until the monster began to tire and slunk away.

The next day, the beast returned. The same thing happened and the monster again grew tired and this time flapped its wings and flew away.

On the third day, Jack made a camel drink several barrels of water. When the dragon appeared, Jack made the camel spit out its water to put out the fire. Then Jack went in for the kill, stabbing the beast. The princess, and all her people, were saved.

Jack and the princess were betrothed, and Jack went away for some more adventures.

After nine months, the princess had a baby, but no one knew who was the father. The king was angry with his daughter, but they went to see a fairy, who might give them the answer. The fairy placed a lemon in the child's hand and said, "Only the child's father will be able to remove this fruit."

The king then called all the men in his kingdom to the palace and each one tried to take away the lemon. But no matter how hard they tried, the fruit would not come away from the baby's hand.

104

Finally, Jack appeared, and as soon as he touched the baby, the lemon came away.

The king was angry with Jack and his daughter, and wanted them to leave the palace. He put them in rags, set them in a rotten boat and cast them out to sea. The couple thought that their boat was about to sink when a lady appeared. "I was the fairy who gave Jack his sword, and protected the princess from the breath of the beast," she said. "I will help you." She repaired the boat, gave them fine robes, and so they returned to the palace.

Jack explained to the king who he was. "I saved your daughter from the monster," said Jack. Then Jack produced the king's gold cup and the head of the monster. Then the princess showed him the ringlet of stones in Jack's hair. Convinced of the truth, the king allowed the couple to marry. They lived in great happiness, and eventually, Jack became king.

Kate Crackernuts

Long ago there lived a king and a queen. Each had
a daughter; the king's daughter, Kate, was fairer than
the queen's daughter, and the queen was jealous of
her. The queen plotted a way to spoil Kate's beauty.

The queen visited a witch, who told her to stop
Kate from eating and to send the girl to her. The
queen sent Kate to the witch to ask for some eggs,
but Kate had a bite to eat before she left the house.
When Kate arrived, the witch told her to lift the
lid off a pot. But nothing happened. "Tell your
mother to keep the larder locked," said the witch.

The next morning. Kate went to the witch. On her
way she saw some people picking peas. Kate had
some peas to eat, so once more nothing happened
when the witch asked Kate to open the pot.

The next day the queen went with Kate. When Kate
lifted the lid of the pot, the head of a sheep changed
places with Kate's own head. The queen was satisfied.

The queen's daughter was sorry for Kate. She put a cloth over Kate's head and they set out to see if anyone could cure her. The two girls went far until Kate's sister did not feel well, so they tried to find lodgings in a castle which belonged to a king. They knocked on the door, and the guards let them in.

Once inside the castle courtyard, the girls told the people they were travelers far away from home and asked if they could have lodgings for the night. They were soon granted their wish, as long as Kate stayed up

at night to look after the king's sick son. Kate was promised a purse of silver, and she agreed.

At midnight the castle clock struck twelve and the prince climbed out of bed. He put on his clothes, opened the door of his room, and went downstairs to the stables. Kate followed, making sure that she wasn't seen even when she jumped silently up on the horse behind him.

As they rode through a forest Kate picked nuts from the trees. When they reached a green hill, the prince stopped his horse. "Open and let the prince enter," said the king's son. "And his lady too," said Kate, quietly.

An opening appeared and they rode in. Kate saw a fine hall, filled with dancing lords and ladies.

Kate watched some fairies and a child playing with a wand. "Three strokes of the wand will make Kate's sister well," said a fairy. So Kate rolled nuts across the floor to the child until he forgot the wand, and Kate hid it in her apron.

When a cock crew, the prince mounted his horse, and with Kate behind they rode back to the castle. As soon as she could, Kate tapped her sister three times with the wand, and she was better. Then Kate's sister touched Kate with the wand, and the sheep's head disappeared. Kate's fair face returned. Kate then sat by the fire, cracking nuts and eating them as if nothing had happened. When the king asked her how she had fared with his son, she replied that he had had a good night.

The king asked her to sit with him one night more, and he offered her a purse of gold pieces in payment if she would agree.

So the next night Kate once more sat by the prince's bedside. When the clock struck midnight, the prince went to his horse and rode again to the green hill, as before.

The king asked Kate to watch his son for one night more. "How shall I reward you this time?" asked the king.

"Let me marry your son if I look after him for a third night."

As on the two previous nights, the prince went to his horse at midnight and rode to the green hill. Kate sat quietly as the prince danced. Once more, she noticed the small child who had had the wand. This time, he was playing with a bird, and Kate heard one of the fairies say, "Three bites of that bird would cure the prince."

So Kate rolled nuts across the
floor to the child until he had
forgotten the bird, and Kate
hid it in her apron.

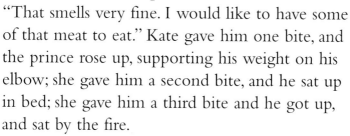

They returned to the castle,
and instead of cracking her
nuts as before, Kate plucked
the bird and roasted it. When he
smelled the bird, the prince said
"That smells very fine. I would like to have some
of that meat to eat." Kate gave him one bite, and
the prince rose up, supporting his weight on his
elbow; she gave him a second bite, and he sat up
in bed; she gave him a third bite and he got up,
and sat by the fire.

When the king and the others came into the
room they found the prince and Kate cracking
nuts and eating them together. The prince looked
as well as could be, and soon they were married.
Meanwhile, the king's other son married the
queen's daughter. They all lived in happiness, and
were never again troubled by royal jealousy.

The Son of the King of Ireland

One day the King of Ireland's son was hunting, and
brought down a raven. He looked at the bird's
black feathers and red blood, and thought, "I will
not marry until I find a woman with hair as black
and cheeks as red as this raven's."

When he got home he told his father, who
replied, "You will not easily find such a woman."

The youth said, "I will travel the world until I do."

So the son of the King of Ireland set off on his
search. Everywhere he went, he asked people if
they had seen a woman with hair as black and
cheeks as red as the raven's. And he was told that
the King of the Great World had three daughters,
and that the youngest was just such a woman.

On his way to find her, the lad called on a smith,
who was making a great needle. "You are in luck,"
said the smith. "This needle I am making is for the

King of the Great World himself. I will ask his men to ferry you across to his castle tomorrow."

The boat came in the morning and when they arrived at the castle, the lad, dusty with travel, went straight to the King of the Great World, to ask him for one of his daughters in marriage.

"If you want to marry my daughter, you must be of nobler birth than you look," said the king.

"I am the son of the King of Ireland," said the boy.

The King of the Great World paused. "You must do three things to win the hand of my daughter," he said. "First, clear my great barn, make it so clean that a gold ball will run across the floor."

The youth started, but no matter how much he cleaned, it still stayed dirty. Just then, the king's three daughters came by. They could see that the lad was harassed and could not finish his task.

Two daughters said, "If we thought you wanted either of us, we would clear the barn for you."

But the youngest daughter said, "Whether you want me or not, I will clear the barn." She said, "Clean, clean, pitchfork, put out shovel." Straight away the whole floor of the barn was clean.

When the king returned, he said he was pleased with the boy's work and told him his next task. "Tomorrow you must thatch the barn with birds' feathers, with the stem of every feather pointing inwards and the roof to be tied with a silk thread."

But the wind blew the feathers away. Then, the king's three daughters came by. Two daughters said, "If we thought you wanted either of us, we would thatch the barn for you."

But the youngest daughter said, "Whether you want me or not, I will thatch the barn." She took out her whistle and blew. Straightaway, a beautiful,

thatch of birds' feathers covered the roof of the barn, just as the king had ordered.

The king said, "I am pleased with your work. But I am not pleased with your teacher. Tomorrow you must mind my five swans. Let any of them escape, and you will be hanged, but if you keep them, you shall have my daughter."

The swans kept escaping. Then, the king's three daughters came by. Two daughters said, "If we thought you wanted either of us, we would find the swans for you." But the youngest daughter said, "Whether you want me or not, I will find them." When she blew her whistle the swans came home.

115

When the King of the Great World arrived, the lad said, "Shall I get your daughter now?"

"No," replied the king. "Tomorrow I am going fishing. You must clean and cook the fish I catch."

The next day the son of the King of Ireland began to clean the fish. But no matter how many scales he removed, more appeared in their place. Just then, the king's three daughters came by. Two daughters said, "If we thought you wanted either of us, we would clean and cook the fish for you." But the youngest daughter said, "If you want me or not, son of the King of Ireland, I will clean the fish."

And she did, saying, "My father will kill us both when he wakens. We must take flight together." The pair took flight, and galloped off together.

Soon the king leapt on his horse, and gave chase. The lad and the princess heard the horse's hooves beating on the ground behind them. The daughter said, "See what you can find in the horse's ear."

"Just a little bit of thorn," said the lad.

"Throw it behind you," said the girl. The thorn grew into a dense wood. The king could not get through, until he hacked himself a path.

Again the daughter said, "Look in the horse's ear."

"There's a tiny stone," he said.

"Throw it behind you," she replied. The stone turned into a massive rock, seven miles long and one mile high, and the couple were on the top.

The king had to return home, and the couple went on their way to Ireland. As they approached the palace of the King of Ireland, the girl said, "I will not come in now. When you go in, the dog will jump up to welcome you. Keep him away, if the dog touches your face, you will forget me."

The couple went their separate ways. The daughter wore men's clothes and lived with a smith as an apprentice. After a year she was his best apprentice.

One day the smith and his apprentice were invited to the wedding of the son of the King of Ireland to the King of Farafohuinn's daughter. "I must use the smithy tonight," said the daughter and she made a hen of gold and a silver cockerel.

The smith and his apprentice left for the wedding, she with the golden hen and silver cockerel, he with some grains of wheat. Someone asked what they could do to entertain the guests. They put the golden hen and the silver cockerel on the floor and threw down three grains of wheat. The cockerel picked up two grains, the hen only one.

"Do you remember when I cleaned the great barn? If you remembered, you would not take two grains instead of one," said the hen.

Everyone laughed, and threw down another three grains. "Remember the thatch I made with birds' feathers?" asked the hen.

They threw down more grains, and the son of the King of Ireland remembered what had happened to him.

"Remember how I found the swans for you? If so, you would not take two grains instead of one."

Now the king's son was sure. "It must be you," he shouted, and found that under the apprentice's costume she was indeed a woman.

The son of the King of Ireland turned to the princess of Farafohuinn, and said "I went in search of this woman. I passed through many tests and trials for her. I will marry none but her. Stay and celebrate with us, but otherwise you may go."

The princess of Farafohuinn left the castle. The Son of the King of Ireland married his true love.

The Greek Princess and the Young Gardener

There was once an old king with one daughter. The king grew ill and it seemed as if the end of his life was coming, but he discovered that the apples from his garden made him better. So the king became angry when a strange, brightly colored bird flew into his garden one evening and began to steal the apples.

The king called his gardener. "You must guard my apple tree day and night, for a bird is coming into the garden and stealing all the fruit."

"I will set my three sons to guard the tree. And if the bird comes near, they will shoot it with their bows and arrows," replied the gardener.

The gardener's eldest son stood guard by the apple tree. The night went on and soon he was asleep at the foot of the tree. At midnight, the bird flew into the garden and removed an apple.

The king heard the bird, for he was a light sleeper, and dashed to his window. The bird was taking off with the finest apple in his beak. "Wake up!" he shouted at the gardener's son. The lad grabbed his bow and arrow, but the bird had got away.

The next night, the gardener's second son was on guard. Again the lad was asleep when the bird came to steal an apple. Again the king roared at the gardener's boy, but the bird had flown away, and another of the king's finest, most succulent apples was gone from the tree. The king began to despair.

On the third evening, it was the youngest son's turn. He was determined to gain credit with the king. As usual the bird arrived and the boy let loose one arrow at the bird as it flew. The bird did not fall, but as the arrow fell, one of the bird's feathers fell too. The king was pleased, for the bird had not had the chance to steal an apple, and the king was fascinated by the feather. It was made of the finest beaten gold. The king decided to catch the bird with the golden feathers. He offered half his kingdom, plus the hand of his daughter in marriage, to any man who capture the bird.

All the young men of the king's household, including the gardener's sons, wondered how they could find the bird. The gardener's first son was out one day when he met a fox. "If you want to find the golden bird," said the fox, "go along this road and take lodging with the poor man and his wife."

So the boy went along the road, but opposite the poor man's house was a house with people drinking and dancing, and the gardener's first son went there for some fun.

The same thing happened to the gardener's second son, and he joined his brother.

When the third son met the fox, the animal gave him the same advice. Unlike his brothers, the young lad listened to what the fox had to say, and sought lodgings with the poor couple, and the next morning went on his way. Soon he met the fox once more. "Well done for taking my advice," said the fox. "Do you know where to find the golden bird?"

"I have no idea," said the young man.

"She is in the palace of the King of Spain, some two hundred miles from here," said the fox.

The gardener's son was sad to hear that the journey was to be so long. "Do not despair," said the fox. "Hop on my tail, we shall soon be there."

So off they went. To the young gardener's surprise, they soon got to the King of Spain's palace. The fox turned to the lad again and told him where in the palace to find the golden bird. "Get the bird out quickly, and do not look for other treasure," said the fox. "Then you will be safe."

The youth entered the palace and found the bird in a dull iron cage. Next to it was a fine golden cage, which the lad thought would be a better home for the marvellous bird. So he tried to tempt the creature into the golden cage. But all that happened was that the bird let out a terrible squeal, and the palace guards came running. Soon, the boy found himself in front of the King of Spain himself.

"I should hang you for a thief," said the king. "But you have a chance to win your life, and the golden bird too. Get me the bay filly belonging to the King of Morocco, a horse that runs faster than any other. Then you shall have the golden bird."

The young man found his friend the fox, and they went on their way to find the King of Morocco.

They arrived and the fox spoke sternly to the lad.
"When you get into the stables, do not touch a
thing. Lead out the bay filly, and all will be well."

When he entered the stable, the boy saw a fine
golden saddle, much better than the leather one
on the filly's back, so he decided to change it over.
But palace guards appeared from every quarter,
and the King of Morocco himself soon arrived.

"I should hang you for a thief," said the king.
"But there is one thing that I want, and if you
help me, then I will let you go, and the bay filly

with you." The king explained that he wanted to marry Golden Locks, the daughter of the King of Greece, and asked the gardener's boy to go to Greece and bring back the princess.

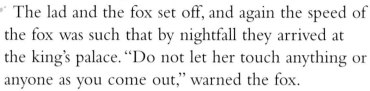

The lad and the fox set off, and again the speed of the fox was such that by nightfall they arrived at the king's palace. "Do not let her touch anything or anyone as you come out," warned the fox.

The lad found the princess and quietly explained why he wanted to take her to Morocco. At first, she was unwilling go with him, but as she looked at the young gardener, her heart began to melt and she agreed. "Only let me kiss my father goodbye," she said. The princess promised not to waken him, but as soon as her lips touched her father's he let out a great cry, and guards came running.

The king listened to the young gardener's story. He was sad to let his daughter go. "I will only let her go if you will clear up the great heap of clay in front of my palace," said the king. The heap had got larger every time a shovel of clay that was removed.

To everyone's great astonishment, including that

of the young gardener, the pile of clay was cleared. The lad knew that the fox had something to do with it. So the young gardener, the princess and the fox went on their way.

By the time they arrived at the King of Morocco's palace, the young gardener and the princess were in love. The king brought out his bay filly in exchange for the princess, and the pair looked longingly at each other. "Please let me say farewell to the princess before I depart," said the lad. When the king was distracted, the pair jumped up on the horse and rode off to the King of Spain's palace where the fox was waiting for them.

127

Before they entered the palace the fox said, "If you give the king the filly, I will have to carry you all home. I am not strong enough, so when you hand over the horse, go up to the creature and stroke it, as if you are saying farewell. When the king is distracted, jump on the filly's back and ride away at top speed."

The king brought out the golden bird, and gave it to the gardener's boy. Then, to his amazement, the boy rode the filly out of the palace gates where the boy met up with the fox and the princess again, and the three returned to the home of the young gardener.

They reached the spot where the lad and the fox first met, and he turned to the creature to thank him for all his help. "Now will you help me?" asked the fox. "Take your sword and chop off my head and tail." The young man could not do this to his friend, but his eldest brother, who knew nothing about the fox, dealt the two blows.

A young man appeared and the Greek princess recognized her brother, who had been bewitched.

The Greek princess and the young gardener were overjoyed, and they longed to share their joy with the king. So the three of them went to see the old king and his daughter, gave the king his golden bird, and told them the whole story. The Greek princess married the young gardener, and the Greek prince married the daughter of the old king. The king was so enchanted with his golden bird that he even shared with it some of the apples from his favorite tree.

Canobie Dick

Canobie Dick was a horse trader who was well known for getting the best deal. Regardless of who he dealt with, he got more than he paid for every piece of horse-flesh that passed through his hands.

One night Dick was riding home across Bowden Moor by the Eildon Hills with two horses that he had not been able to sell, when he saw a figure coming towards him. As the man got nearer, Dick saw that he was an old fellow, wearing ancient clothes. To Dick's surprise the old man greeted him and asked if the horses were for sale. They struck a deal, and the old man paid Dick a good price in old gold coins. Normally Dick would have refused these, but he knew that gold was valuable in any form, so he took the payment readily.

A few times more Dick met the man and sold him horses, the old man always asking that Dick come at night to make the sale. When this had happened several times, Dick decided that he should get to know this customer better. He said to the man, "A bargain is luckier when struck with a glass in hand."

So the old man invited Dick to his home, but warned him, "Don't be afraid at what you see in my dwelling-place, for if you do you'll be sorry for the rest of your life."

They went on a narrow path up the hills and came to a rocky outcrop. The old man suddenly passed through a passage into the hillside which Dick had never noticed before.

"You are sure you are not afraid?" asked the old man. "It is not

131

too late to turn back if you've changed your mind."

Dick shook his head – he did not wish to seem frightened. Flaming torches lit the passage, and Dick saw a long row of stables, each with a black horse. Next to each horse lay a knight in black armor. On an old table was a horn and a sword.

"The man that blows this horn and draws this sword shall become king of the whole of Britain," said the man.

Dick was fascinated. He lifted the sword briefly, but put it down again. When he thought of the knights and the horses, he thought that drawing the sword might bring alive all these terrors. So he raised the horn to his lips and got ready to blow.

Dick was so frightened that all he could produce was a feeble note. But this was enough to rouse the knights. Thunder echoed in the hall, the horses came to life and the knights rose up. The horses began to neigh and stamp their hooves, tossing their heads in excitement.

To the horse dealer it looked as if the army coming to life around him was about to attack. Trembling, he dropped the horn, and grabbed the great sword on the table. As he did so, a mighty voice spoke from among the knights:

The coward shall rue the day he was born
Who lay down the sword and blew on the horn.

Dick was picked up by a whirlwind that cast him out onto hillside. There he lay unconscious until a group of shepherds found him in the morning.

Dick told the shepherds his tale, but died soon afterwards. And no one found the passage into the hillside again.

The Knight of Riddles

Once there was a king called Ardan, king of all Albann whose first wife died. Some time later he remarried, and the king had two sons, one from each queen. The two boys were very close, but the new queen was jealous of the king's first son. She knew that her own boy would not inherit the kingdom and so she plotted to kill the elder son.

Twice the queen ordered a poisoned drink for the elder son, and twice her own son overheard her orders, and warned his brother. Then the elder son said to his brother, "I shall not live long if I stay here, it will be better for me to leave." And so the two brothers decided to leave together.

They took their mother's poisonous drink in a bottle, and before long, the eldest said, "It might not be poison, let's try it on my horse." They gave the poison to the beast, and it keeled over and died.

"Well, she was a tired old nag anyway," said the elder brother. "Her time was up. Let's try the drink

on your steed." So they did and the horse died.

The brothers decided to skin the horse to make a blanket to keep themselves warm. While did this, twelve ravens flew down to feast on the carcass. But the birds died from the poisoned meat.

The brothers took the dead birds with them and found a baker. They asked him to make twelve pies from the ravens' flesh and took the pies on their journey. One night the brothers were set upon by twenty-four robbers. "Give us your money!" demanded the thieves.

"We have no money," said the brothers. "All we have are these meat pies."

"That is as good as money. We'll take them."

Greedily, the robbers began to eat the pies and soon they fell down dead, poisoned by the meat. When the brothers came to a fine house, the home of the Knight of Riddles, they decided to visit the knight, and the younger brother pretended to be the servant to the elder.

The Knight of Riddles had a beautiful daughter with twelve maidens. No one was allowed to marry the girl unless they could give him a riddle he could not solve. The brothers put this riddle to him: "One killed two, and two killed twelve, and twelve killed twenty-four, and two got out of it."

The knight tried to answer the riddle. Meanwhile each maiden came to the younger brother with gifts and asked him the riddle's answer. "Only my brother may tell the answer," he said.

Then the knight's daughter went to the elder brother and, smiling at him, presented him with a gift of cloth, and he told her the riddle's answer. The knight then called the brothers to him and told them that he had solved the riddle.

"Your riddle was easy to solve," said the knight. "Your head will be chopped off in the morning."

"Before you behead me," said the elder brother, "I have another riddle. My servant and I were in the forest shooting. He shot twelve hares, skinned them, and let them go. Then came a hare finer than the rest. I shot her, skinned her, and let her go."

"That's not a difficult riddle," said the knight. And they all knew that the young man had discovered how the knight found the answers to his riddles, and the knight was defeated in the battle of the riddles. So the elder brother married his daughter. The elder prince told his brother to go home and inherit his kingdom while he stayed in the land of the Knight of the Riddles.

The elder brother was well liked, especially when he killed three fearsome giants. The Knight of the Riddles gave him a title, Hero of the White Shield.

The Hero of the White Shield was famed as the strongest and bravest man in the land. Many challenged him to a fight, but no one beat him.

One day, a stranger challenged him. After a long fight, the Hero jumped in alarm over a stone wall.

"You must have some of my own fighting blood in your veins to be so strong," said the Hero of the White Shield. "What is your family?"

"I'm the son of Ardan, king of all Albann," replied the stranger. It was the Hero of the White Shield's long-lost brother. The two stayed together for years, but eventually the younger brother had to return to his own land.

On the way home, the younger brother stopped to watch twelve men playing. The smallest of the twelve grappled with him and shook him as if he were no more than a child. "Whose sons are you, who are so strong?" he asked.

"We are the nephews of the Hero of the White Shield," they cried. The younger brother knew he had found his sons, and that all were alive and well. They went together to find his wife, and a great celebration was held. For hundreds of years, the kings of Albann were descended from their line.

The Humble-Bee

Two young men were out walking one summer's day and stopped by a stream next to an old ruined house. They noticed how the stream turned into a miniature waterfall crossed by narrow blades of grass. They sat down by the stream and soon one was fast asleep, and the other sat watching the view.

Suddenly, a creature, the size of a humble-bee, flew out of the sleeper's mouth. It walked over grass stalks to cross the stream and then disappeared into the ruin through one of the cracks in the wall.

The man who saw all this was shocked and went to shake his companion awake. Then he saw the tiny creature emerge from the ruin, fly across the stream and re-enter the sleeper's mouth, just as the young man was waking.

"What's the matter? Are you ill?" asked the watcher.

"I am well," replied the sleeper. "You have just interrupted the most wonderful dream, and I wish you had not woken me with your shaking.

I dreamed that I walked through a grassy plain to a wide river. I wanted to see what was on the other side, and I found a silver bridge near a great waterfall. I walked over the bridge and on the far bank was a beautiful palace built of stone. The chambers of the palace contained great mounds of gold and jewels. I was looking at all these fine things, wondering at the wealth of the person who left them there, and deciding which to bring away with me. Then suddenly you woke me, and I could bring away none of the riches."

The Seal Woman

There was an unmarried farmer from Wastness.
Friends teased him when he said he had no interest
in women, but he took no notice. His only interest
was his farm, and the good farmer grew rich.

One day the farmer was walking by the shore at
the ebb tide, and noticed a group of seal folk
sunning themselves on a rock and swimming in the
sea. The seals did not notice the farmer, so he crept
closer and saw that they had all taken off their
sealskins and their bodies were as pale as his own.

The farmer thought it would be fun to catch one
of the naked seals, so he edged closer and then

made a dash for the seals. They grabbed their skins in alarm and jumped into the water, but the farmer managed to hold on to one of the skins.

He watched the seals swim out to sea and then turned to walk home. He heard sobbing behind him, and turned to see a seal-woman, weeping for her lost skin. "I cannot join my family in the sea without it," she cried.

The farmer felt pity, but he was also smitten by the beauty of the seal woman. He talked to her, and told her his feelings. Soon he persuaded her to come ashore and live with him as his wife.

She lived long with the farmer and was a good farmer's wife. She bore him seven children, four boys and three girls. She sang and seemed happy, but she sometimes looked with longing at the sea.

One day the farmer took his three eldest sons out in his boat to go fishing. The seal-woman sent three children to gather limpets and whelks. The youngest daughter stayed at home, because the girl's foot was sore and she could not walk far.

Once they had all gone out the seal-woman started to search the house. Her daughter realized that she was looking for something, and asked her mother what it was.

"Tell no one," said the seal woman. "I am looking for a fine skin to make a dressing for your foot."

The young girl replied, "I might know where you can find one. When you were out one day and father thought we were asleep, I saw him take a skin and look at it. Then he folded it carefully and hid it away up in the eaves above the bed."

The seal woman rushed to the eaves. "Farewell my little one," she said, as she ran with the skin in the direction of the shore. She put on her skin, dived into the sea, and swam away. A male seal saw her coming and greeted her with excitement, for he recognized the seal he had loved long ago.

As the farmer was returning to shore in his boat, he saw his wife diving into the sea and swimming to the male seal. "Farewell, dear husband," she called to him. "I liked you well and you treated me kindly. But it is time that I returned to my true love of the sea."

That was the last the farmer saw of the seal woman. He missed his seal-wife greatly, and it took him many years to recover from his sadness. And he often went for walks along the shore, hoping to catch sight of her again.

145

Rashen Coatie

There was a king whose queen died young, and after a time he remarried. The couple both had a daughter from their first marriage. His daughter, Rashen Coatie, was good and beautiful, while her daughter was ill-featured and bad-tempered.

The queen treated the king's daughter badly so that her own girl would gain. To keep the peace, her husband turned a blind eye to this ill-treatment, and Rashen Coatie ended up looking after the king's cattle, while the queen's daughter stayed at home and wallowed in luxury.

The queen sent bad food for Rashen Coatie to eat to make the girl fall ill and die, but a fairy taught Rashen Coatie a spell. If she said the magic words, a calf appeared with food as fine as any that was eaten in the king's palace. In this way, Rashen Coatie became stronger and more beautiful than ever, and the queen became angrier and angrier.

When her plan failed, the queen went to talk to a witch. The queen was given the power to look into the unknown, and she realized that it was the calf who was giving Rashen Coatie her food.

She asked her husband to have the calf killed, so that she might cook the animal for a banquet, and the king agreed. Rashen Coatie was distressed to hear what was to happen, but the calf spoke in her ear. "Do as I say and you need not worry," said the calf. "When I am cooked and eaten, bury my bones under this stone, then leave the palace for a

147

while, and then you will be safe."

Rashen Coatie did as instructed and went into hiding. The calf came back to life and brought her food, and so she survived. The queen was poisoned after eating the calf meat, and eventually died.

Rashen Coatie grew into a fine young woman and decided to return to her father's court in disguise. But this caused confusion because her father was so taken with her beauty that he wanted to marry her. She asked the calf what to do.

"Ask the king for clothes made of the rushes that grow by the stream," said the calf. A dress was made, and the king still wanted to marry Rashen Coatie.

"Ask the king for a dress of all the colors of the birds of the air," said the calf. This was done, and still he wanted to marry her.

"Ask the king for a dress, with the colors of all the fish of the sea," said the calf. But again the king produced just such a dress, and still he wanted to marry Rashen Coatie.

Finally the girl could find no more excuses, and the wedding day arrived. When she got to church,

Rashen Coatie tried one last objection. "I must
have the ring my mother wore when she was
married," she said. Then she put on her dress of
rushes, and ran from her father's kingdom.

After long wandering, Rashen Coatie came to a
prince's hunting lodge and collapsed in a deep
sleep on the prince's bed. Later, the prince himself
arrived and found Rashen Coatie on his bed. He
asked her what she was doing there. "I am far from
home, tired and lost. Is there somewhere I might
find work?" So the prince took Rashen Coatie
home and put her to work in the palace kitchens.

Soon it was Christmas and all the people in the palace went to church in the morning. Rashen Coatie was left behind to turn the roasting spits.

She wanted to go to church, and decided to use a spell so the spits would turn themselves:

Every spit turn on your way
Until I return on this yule day.

And with that, Rashen Coatie put on her finest dress and ran off to church.

In church, the prince was entranced by the beautiful young woman who entered just as the

service was beginning. Little did he guess that it was the kitchen maid, Rashen Coatie. The prince decided to speak to her as she left the church, but she slipped back to the palace, hoping that none would know that she had left the kitchen.

But as the girl flew along, she left one of her tiny golden shoes. The prince said "The woman whose foot fits this shoe shall be my bride," he said.

Hundreds of women tried the show but it fitted no-one. The witch's daughter had pared her nails and rubbed some of the skin off her heels, and she squeezed on the shoe. True to his word the prince announced that he would marry the girl. But a small bird fluttered over the prince's head, singing:

Clipped the heel and pared the toe;
In the kitchen the shoe will go.

The prince turned back and ran to the kitchen, finding Rashen Coatie, who had not tried on the shoe. When it fitted, the prince went to church with his rightful bride.

The Tale of Ivan

Ivan was a poor man who had no work and so one day he left his wife to look for a job. After a while he came to a farm and the farmer agreed to take Ivan on and give him lodgings.

Ivan worked for a year, then the master said, "Ivan, you have worked well this year and now you must be paid. Will you take money or advice?"

"I prefer to have my wages in money," said Ivan.

"I would prefer to give you advice," said the master. "Never leave the old road for the new one."

Ivan worked for his master another year.

At the end of the second year, the same thing happened. The master told Ivan, "Never lodge where an old man is married to a young woman."

After a third year, Ivan had a third piece of advice, "Honesty is the best policy." By now, Ivan saw that he would get no money, so he decided to return to his wife. Maybe there would be work nearer home.

"Very well," said the master. "I will give you a cake to eat on your journey."

Ivan set off and soon met a group of merchants who were returning home from a fair. He got on well with the merchants, but when they came to a fork in the road, the men wanted to travel along the shorter, straighter, new road. Ivan remembered his master's first piece of advice. "I prefer the old road," said Ivan, and they parted company.

Before long, the merchants were set upon by robbers. Ivan could see what was happening from the old road and he bellowed "Robbers! Stop thief!" When the robbers heard this, they ran off, and the merchants kept hold of their money.

Eventually, the two roads joined again near a market town, and Ivan met the merchants once more. They thanked him for saving them from the robbers and offered to pay for a night's lodgings.

"I'll see the host first," said Ivan, and he found out that the inn was run by an old man with a young wife. Remembering his master's advice, he said "I'll not lodge here, I will stay next door."

The young wife of the old landlord was plotting with a young monk to kill her husband and take over the inn. If they did the crime that night they could blame the merchants, the only guests and so they prepared to carry out the wicked plan. But they did not know that Ivan, getting ready to go to bed in his room next door, could hear through the wall. There was a missing pine knot in the wall and Ivan looked through and saw them talking.

Suddenly, the young woman saw the hole in the wall. "Block that hole," she said, "someone may see."

So the monk stood against the hole while the wicked woman stabbed her husband to death.

Ivan took his knife and cut a piece of the monk's habit while he stood against the hole.

Next morning, the crime was discovered. "It must have been that gang of wicked merchants staying at the inn," the wife cried. And so the merchants were marched off to prison, and Ivan saw them pass.

"Woe to us, Ivan!" they cried. "We are taken for this murder, but we are all innocent."

"I will find the real murderers," called Ivan.

"If I cannot bring them to justice let them hang *me* for the murder."

So Ivan went to the justices and told them all he had heard. At first, the justices did not believe him, but he showed them the piece of cloth he had cut from the monk's robe, and the young wife and the monk were arrested. The merchants were released, thanked Ivan, and went on their way.

When Ivan got home to his wife she ran to greet him. "You come in the nick of time," she said. "I have just found a fine purse of gold. It has no name on it, but it must belong to the lord of the manor."

Ivan remembered the third piece of advice and said "Honesty is the best policy.".

They went to the lord's castle and left the purse with the servant at the gatehouse.

One day when the lord passed Ivan's house, his wife mentioned the purse to him. "I know of no purse returned to me," said the lord, in puzzlement. "Surely my servant must have kept it for himself." So he sought out the servant. When the servant saw that he was found out he gave up the purse.

The lord frowned at his wicked servant. "I have no use for dishonesty. Be gone," he ordered.

Then the lord asked Ivan. "Will you be my servant in his place?"

"Thank you," said Ivan. He and his wife were given fine new quarters in the castle. When they were moving in, Ivan remembered the cake his old master had given him. They cut themselves a piece, and out fell three gold coins, Ivan's wages for his work for his old master. "Truly, honesty is the best policy," laughed Ivan.

And his wife agreed.

157

Cherry of Zennor

Near the village of Zennor in Cornwall there
lived a man everyone called Old Honey, in a tiny
two-room hut with his wife and ten children.
They grew food on the land around the hut, and
gathered limpets and periwinkles from the shore.

Old Honey's favorite daughter was Cherry, who
could run as fast as the wind. She was mischievous,
but had such a winning smile that everyone liked
her. She loved to steal the horse of the miller's boy,
and would ride out to the cliffs. If the miller's boy
started to catch up, she left the horse behind, hid
in the rocks or cairns that there were along the
coast, and was never caught or found.

Cherry was a sweet-natured child until she
reached her teens. She wanted to have a new dress,
so that she could cut a fine figure at church or at
the fair. But there was no money for dresses, so she
mended the one she had. She thought it was not fit
for her to go to the fair and look for a sweetheart.

One day, Cherry decided to leave home to look for a job so that she might have money of her own. The next morning she made a bundle of her few possessions and set off. She trudged along, but when she came to the Lady Downs cross roads, she sat down on a stone and cried. She felt tired, missed her family, and wished she was not alone.

Just as she was drying her eyes and deciding that she would return to her family, a gentleman appeared. Cherry thought this was odd, since she had seen no one coming before, and on the Downs you could see for miles around.

When the man bid her "Good morning," Cherry told him why she had left home, but that she had lost heart and was going to return.

"I did not expect such luck," said the man. "I am looking for a young woman to keep house for me, for I am recently widowed." So Cherry decided to go with the man, and they set off together.

The old man explained that his home was in the "low country", not far away. They reached an area where the lanes were sunk deep into the ground, with trees and bushes high on either side. Little sunlight reached the lane, but the rich scent of sweetbrier and honeysuckle reassured Cherry, who might have been afraid of the dark.

When they came to a river the gentleman carried Cherry across. On the other side, the lane seemed even darker, and Cherry held the man's arm.

When they came to the gentleman's home, Cherry could not believe her eyes. The dark lane had not prepared her for a place of such beauty. The garden was full of flowers of every color, fruit of all descriptions hung down from the trees, and birds sat in the branches, singing as if they were pleased that the master of the house was home.

The garden was so unlike her own home that Cherry remembered how her grandmother had told her of places that had been enchanted by the little people. Could this be such a place?

Cherry looked up as a voice called "Papa!" and a small child, about two years old, came rushing towards the gentleman. But when Cherry looked at the child, although he was small, his faced seemed old and wrinkled. A haggard old woman appeared from the house and came towards them.

"This is Aunt Prudence, grandmother of my late wife," said the gentleman. He explained that once Cherry knew her work, grandmother would leave.

Cherry found that inside the house was even more beautiful than the garden. Aunt Prudence produced a large and tasty meal, then the old woman showed Cherry to her room.

"Keep your eyes closed in bed," said Aunt Prudence. "Or you may see things that frighten you." Then she explained that in the morning Cherry was to take the boy to the spring, wash him and then rub ointment into his eyes. The ointment was in a box hidden in a gap in the rock by the spring. On no account should she put the ointment on her own eyes. Then she was to milk the cow, and give the boy milk for his breakfast.

Next morning, Cherry rose early and began her work. She took the little boy to the spring, washed him and put the ointment on his eyes. But she could not see the cow. So Cherry made the clicking noise which she had used to call in the cows at home, and suddenly a fine cow appeared from the

trees, and Cherry sat down to milk her.

After breakfast, the old woman showed Cherry the kitchen, then Aunt Prudence told Cherry that under no circumstances should she go into any of the locked rooms. "You might see something that would frighten you," she repeated.

Cherry went to help her master in the garden. She liked the gentleman, but Cherry did not like the old woman, who hovered in the background, muttering as if she wanted Cherry gone.

When Cherry seemed settled in her new home, Prudence said, "Now you shall see some parts of the house you have not seen before." One room had a floor polished like glass and around the walls were figures of men, women, and children, all made of stone. They looked as if they were real people who had somehow been turned to stone, and she shivered with fear as she looked at them.

Cherry thought she was in an evil house, and told the woman she didn't want to see anymore."

But the old woman laughed, pushed Cherry into a room and made her polish a box that looked like a coffin on legs. "Rub harder, harder!" shouted the old woman, and as Cherry rubbed, she heard an awful, chilling wailing sound. The girl fainted as she heard it, and the master burst into the room.

The gentleman threw the old woman out and gave Cherry a soothing drink which made Cherry feel better, and made her forget what she had seen. She knew she was frightened, and that she did not want to go into that part of the house again.

Life was much better for Cherry with the old woman gone. She was happy in her master's house, but still curious about what was going on there.

When her master was out, she decided to try the child's ointment on her eyes. Her eyes burned so she dashed to the pool to splash cool water on them, There she saw hundreds of tiny people at the bottom of the pool – including her master!

With the ointment she could see the little people everywhere, in flowers, swinging in the trees, under blades of grass. She saw her master playing with a host of the little people. One of them, dressed like a queen, was dancing on top of the coffin, and the master kissed her.

Next day, when Cherry and her master were together in the garden, he bent to kiss her. "Kiss the little people like yourself, as you do when you go under the water," Cherry cried, and slapped her master on the face. The gentleman knew then that Cherry had used some of the ointment on her eyes. She would have to leave him for good.

Sadly, they parted. He gave her a bundle of clothes and other fine things, picked up a lantern, and led her away from his garden, along the sunken lanes, and towards the Downs. Then he gave the girl a final kiss, and said with a hint of sadness in

his voice that he was sorry, but that she must be punished for her curiosity. Perhaps he would see her sometimes if she walked upon the Downs.

So Cherry returned to Zennor. Her people were surprised to see her, for she had been away for so long that they had thought she was dead. Her parents could not believe her story at first, and thought she was covering up some mischief. But Cherry insisted that her story was true, and in time her family accepted what she said. Often she wandered on the Lady Downs, looking for her old master. But she never saw him again.

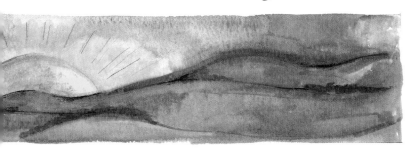

Skillywidden

A man was cutting furze on Trendreen Hill when he saw one of the little people stretched out, fast asleep, on the heath. The man took off the thick cuff that he wore for his work, crept up, and popped the little man into the cuff. He carried him home with care, and put him on to the hearth stone.

When he awoke, the fairy looked quite at home and soon began to enjoy himself playing with the children. They called him Bob of the Heath, and Bob told the man that he would show him where to find crocks of gold hidden on the hillside.

Days later, the neighbors worked to harvest the furze, and then came to the man's house to celebrate with a hearty meal. To keep him from prying eyes, Bob was locked in the barn with the children.

But the fairy and the children were cunning, and found a way out of the barn. Before long they were playing hide-and-seek all around the great heap of furze in the yard.

As they played, they saw a tiny man and woman searching round the furze. "Oh my poor Skillywidden," said the little woman. "Where can you be? Will I ever set eyes on you again?"

Bob told the children to go back indoors. "My parents have come looking for me. I must go back with them." Then he cried, "Here I am Mommy!" And before the children knew it, Bob had vanished with his parents, and they were left in the yard.

Their father was very angry, and beat the children for escaping from the locked barn.

After this the furze-cutter sometimes went to Trendreen Hill to look for fairies and crocks of gold. But he was never able to find either.

I Don't Know

Once, a Duke who lived in Brittany was riding home with his manservant when they saw a young child lying asleep, alone by the side of the road. The Duke was sad to see a boy, about five years old, left by the roadside, so he got down from his horse, went over to the boy, and woke him up.

"Who left you here, my boy?" asked the Duke.

"I don't know."

"Who are your parents?"

"I don't know."

"Which town do you come form?"

"I don't know."

"What are you called?"

"I don't know."

"No one seems to be taking care of you. We will take you home and keep you safe." So the Duke took the child to his castle, and called him N'oun-Doaré, which is the Breton for "I don't know."

N'oun-Doaré grew up with family and was a
healthy, intelligent child. He was sent away to
school and became a handsome young man.

When N'oun-Doaré was eighteen, the Duke
brought him back to live at the castle, and, to show
N'oun-Doaré how pleased he was with his
progress, took him to the local fair to buy him his
own sword and his own horse.

First they went to look for a horse. There were
many horse-dealers at the fair, but N'oun-Doaré
could find no steed that suited him. Then they met
a man leading an old mare and N'oun-Doaré
shouted, "Yes! That is the horse I want!"

The Duke was surprised. "That old nag?" he said.
But the boy insisted.

The horse's owner spoke quietly to N'oun-Doaré. "Your choice is good. See the knots in the mare's mane? Undo one of them, and she will fly fifteen hundred leagues through the air."

Then the Duke and N'oun-Doaré visited the armorer. But again, no sword was right – then N'oun-Doaré saw an old, rusty sword. "That is the sword I would like."

"But you deserve much better than that," said the Duke. "It is old and rusty."

"Please buy it for me; I will put it to good use."

So they bought the old sword. When the lad looked closely at the sword he saw an inscription, almost covered by rust, which said "I am invincible."

N'oun-Doaré could not wait to try a magical flight with his mare, and soon he undid one of the knots in her mane. They flew to Paris, where N'oun-Doaré marveled at the city's sights .
By chance the Duke was also there – he had been called to attend the king. When he met the boy, they went to the royal palace together.
The Duke introduced N'oun-Doaré

to the king, and the lad was given a job looking
after some of the royal stables.

One night, N'oun-Doaré was passing a cross roads
when he saw something glint in the moonlight.
It was a crown with diamonds that shone in the
dark. A voice suddenly said "Be on your guard if
you take it." N'oun-Doaré did not realize, but it
was actually the voice of his old mare. N'oun-
Doaré paused, then took it with him.

He told no one about the crown and hid it in the
stables, but two of the other servants saw it shining
through the keyhole and went to tell the king. The
king took the crown and called all his wise men

about him. But none of them knew where it had come from. There was an inscription on the crown in a strange language which no one could read. Then a child spoke up, saying the crown belonged to the Princess of the Golden Fleece. The king turned to N'oun-Doaré: "Bring me the Princess of the Golden Fleece to be my wife, otherwise you will meet your death."

The lad got on his mare and began to search for the princess, although he had little idea about where to look. He came to a beach, and saw a fish stuck on the sand which seemed to be dying. "Put it in the sea," said the mare, and N'oun-Doaré did so.

"Great thanks to you," said the fish. "You have saved the life of the king of the fish."

Later they came to a bird was trapped in a snare. "Let it go," said the mare, and N'oun-Doaré did so.

"Great thanks to you," said the bird. "You have saved the life of the king of the birds."

Later on their journey they came to a great castle and nearby a man was chained to a tree. "Set him free," said the mare, and N'oun-Doaré did so.

"Great thanks to you.
You have saved the life of
the Demon King."

"Whose castle is this?"
asked N'oun-Doaré.

"It belongs to the Princess
of the Golden Fleece,"
replied the Demon King.

They went into the
castle and N'oun-Doaré
explained why he had
come. The princess was
reluctant to go, but N'oun-
Doaré tricked her on to
his horse, and they flew to
Paris. The king wanted to
marry without delay.

"Before I marry, I must
have my own ring," said
the princess.

N'oun-Doaré was asked
to bring the ring to the

king, but N'oun-Doaré had no idea where to look. Then the mare whispered, "Ask the king of the birds, who you saved. He will help you."

The king of the birds chose the wren, and told her to bring the ring to the princess. "The wren is the best bird for this task," he explained. "She can fly through the keyhole of the princess's chamber."

The wren returned with the ring, and the king wanted to marry straight away. But the princess had another demand. "I need to have my own castle brought to me," she said.

Again, N'oun-Doaré was in despair.

Again, the mare whispered to him, "Ask the Demon King, who you saved. He will help you."

The Demon King set a whole army of demons to work, moving the castle to Paris. Then the princess had one final demand. "I do not have the key to my castle, for it was dropped into the sea when we flew here to Paris on N'oun-Doaré's mare."

N'oun-Doaré saw that this was a task for the king of the fish. Finally, a fish arrived with the diamond-studded key in its mouth.

At last, the Princess agreed to marry the king. The guests were amazed to see N'oun-Doaré take his mare into the church. When the king and princess were married, the mare's skin suddenly vanished, and there stood a beautiful young woman. "Please marry me, N'oun-Doaré," she said. "I am the daughter of the king of Tartary."

N'oun-Doaré and the princess set off to Tartary. People say they lived happily ever after there, but they were never seen in Brittany again.

The Fenoderee

On the Isle of Man lived a fairy who had been sent out of fairyland because he had had a passion for a mortal girl. The fairy folk had found him dancing with his love in the merry Glen of Rushen. When the other fairies heard this, they cast a spell which sent him to the Isle of Man forever, and made him ugly and hairy. And the manx people called him the Fenoderee, which means "hairy one".

Although his appearance was frightening, the Fenoderee was kind to humans, for he never forgot the girl he loved, and wanted to do what he could for her people. Sometimes he used what was left of his fairy magic to carry out tasks which even the strongest of men would have found exhausting.

The Fenoderee liked to help the farmers in their fields. On one occasion he mowed a meadow, but instead of being grateful, the farmer complained that the grass was not short enough.

The Fenoderee still felt sad at losing his mortal love, and was angry with the ungrateful farmer, so next year at mowing time, he let the farmer do the job himself. As the farmer swished his scythe, the Fenoderee crept behind him, cutting up roots, and getting so close to the farmer that he risked having his feet cut off.

When the farmer told this story, people knew they should be grateful when they were helped by the Fenoderee. So the custom arose of leaving the creature little gifts when he had been especially helpful.

THE FENODEREE

Once, a man was building a house of stone. He paid some of the men of the parish to help him quarry it. But there was one large block of fine marble which was too heavy to be moved, even if all the men of the parish tried to shift it.

Next day, to their surprise, the huge block had been carried to the building site, and all the other stone that the builder needed had been moved too.

They wondered how it had happened, then someone said, "It must have been the Fenoderee, working for us in the night." And the builder saw that this must be true.

So as a reward, he took some clothes and left them for him. That night, the Fenoderee appeared and found the clothes. Those who watched him were surprised at his sadness as he lifted each item up in turn and said these words:

Cap for the head, alas, poor head!
Coat for the back, alas, poor back!
Breeches for the breech, alas, poor breech!
If these all be thine, thine cannot be the merry Glen
of Rushen.

With these words, the Fenoderee walked away, and has never been seen since in that neighborhood.

A Bride and a Hero

The Irish used to believe in a faraway land called
Tir na n-Og, the Land of Youth where time went
much more slowly, and people stayed younger
much longer. Every seven years in Tir na n-Og a
race was held and all the strongest men took part.
It began in front of the royal palace and finished at
a hilltop two miles away. A chair was placed on the
summit, and the first runner to sit on it became
king of Tir na n-Og for the next seven years.

There was once a king of Tir na n-Og who was
worried that he would lose his kingdom in the
next race, so he sent for his chief Druid.

"How long shall I win the race and rule this land
before another beats me to the chair?" he asked.

"Have no fear," replied the druid. "Only your own
son-in-law could win the race and take the crown."

The king of Tir na n-Og had an unmarried
daughter, Niamh. So the king decided that to keep

his kingdom he would make his daughter so ugly that no man would marry her. Borrowing his druid's staff, he struck the girl and a pig's head appeared on her shoulders.

The druid was very sorry that he had told the king to beware his son-in-law. He went to Niamh to talk to her.

"Shall I always be like this?" Niamh asked.

"Yes," replied the druid. "You will always look like this unless you go to Ireland and marry one of the sons of Fin."

So Niamh set out for Ireland, hoping to meet one of Fin's sons, and persuade him to marry her. After a while she saw a handsome young man called Oisin, and she was overjoyed when she found out that his father was Fin himself.

One day Oisin was out hunting and killed more game than ever before. At the end of the day, his men were exhausted and hungry, and could carry none of the game home with them, so Oisin was left with his three dogs and a great pile of carcasses. When the men had gone, Niamh stood

by him while he looked at the game. The young man said "I shall be sorry to leave behind some of the meat I have killed today."

"Tie some of the game in a bundle. I will help you carry it," said Niamh. And off they walked together.

When they had talked for a while, Oisin knew Niamh was a fine, caring young woman, and that she would be attractive too, if she did not have a pig's head on her shoulders. Niamh explained that the only way to get back her own head was to come to Ireland marry one of the sons of Fin.

Oisin smiled. "Then you shall not have a pig's head for long," he said.

So Niamh married Oisin, son of Fin. As soon as the ceremony was over, the pig's head vanished, and Niamh's beautiful face returned. When he saw Niamh in her new beauty, Oisin loved her deeply.

After a while Niamh longed to return to the land of Tir na n-Og, and when she told Oisin of her wish, he was keen to go there with her. He knew

it was the land where people never grow old.

When Niamh returned there was great celebration – everyone thought that the princess was lost for ever – and the king lived happily with his daughter and son-in-law.

But soon it was the time for the seven-yearly race to find who should be king. The king and Oisin gathered for the race with all the likely men in the kingdom. Before anyone else was half way up the hill, Oisin was sitting in the seat at the top. It was Oisin's right to be king of Tir na n-Og.

Oisin ruled the Land of Youth for many years and he marveled that he kept his youth. But Oisin missed his Irish homeland and longed to go back for a visit. Niamh warned him, "It will be very dangerous for you if you return to Ireland. Return to your native soil and you will become a blind old man and you will never come home to me."

Oisin could not believe that this would happen.

"How long do you think you have lived with me in Tir na n–Og?" she asked.

"About three years," replied Oisin.

"But they are like three hundred in Ireland."

Niamh could not change Oisin's mind. So Niamh decided to help him. "Ride to Ireland and do not dismount," she said. "You will only lose your youth if you put your own foot on Irish soil. If you leave the saddle, the steed will come back to Tir na n-Og and you will be left, old and blind, in Ireland."

With this warning ringing in his ears, Oisin set off for his homeland on his beautiful white horse. It was rainy and windy, but Oisin was happy to be home once more.

He asked a girl where he might find the house of
Fin and his family. But the girl looked at him with
a puzzled expression. "I know of no such people,"
she said. No one seemed to know who he was
talking about – which was odd, since Fin and his
men had been among the most famous in Ireland.

Finally Oisin asked an old man if he knew the
whereabouts of Fin. "My old grandfather talked of
Fin and his warriors," said the old man. "They lived
in these parts about three hundred years ago."

So Oisin's family were dead. Oisin could still not

188

believe it. Fin's fortress was in ruins and he began
to believe that what the old man said was true, and
that three years in the Land of Youth really were
the same as three hundred mortal years.

Oisin decided to tell the High King of Ireland of
his adventure. On his way, he came across a group
of men who were trying to lift a stone. Fin had
noticed that the men seemed weak and feeble
compared with those in Tir na n-Og, and these
men were no exception. Six of them were tugging
away at the stone, but they could not shift it, let
alone lift it up into the cart that stood waiting

nearby. Oisin stopped to help them and leaned over
to pick up the stone, but Oisin lost his balance.
He reached out to stop himself falling and part of
the stirrup broke. The hero tumbled off his horse
and landed on the floor.

Niamh's warnings ran through his mind. As he
picked himself up he knew they were true; he was

old, stiff, and blind. Niamh's horse trotted away, and Oisin realized that he would never return to Niamh.

Saint Patrick lived nearby, and heard of what had happened. Soon Oisin was brought to Patrick, who gave him a room in his own house, and asked his cook to bring him food every day.

Oisin told Patrick his adventures, with his father Fin and his band of warriors, as well as his adventures in the land of youth. Although he was old and blind, Oisin had a little of his old strength, and sometimes, if Patrick prayed devoutly, Oisin would regain enough energy to help the Saint build his church. And he helped rid Patrick of a monster that came to destroy the building before it was finished.

But Oisin's strength never lasted long. After a while he would be a weak old man again and it was all he could do to eat the food brought to him by Patrick's cook. And so, old and blind, Oisin lived out the last of his days, with only his memories of Tir na n-Og to console him.

The Lazy Beauty

Once upon a time there was a poor widow who had one daughter. The mother was a hard-working women, her house was neat and clean, and used her spinning wheel to make the finest linen thread.

The daughter was a fine-looking girl, but the laziest creature in the town. She got up late, spent ages eating her breakfast, and dawdled around the house doing nothing. Whenever she cooked, she burned herself, whatever she did she knocked something over or broke one of her mother's pots. The girl even drawled her speech, as if it took too much energy to get the words out of her mouth.

One day the widow was giving her daughter a telling off when she heard a horse on the road. It was the king's son riding by. When he heard the woman's voice he stopped to talk to her.

"What is the matter? Is your child so bad that you need to scold her so?"

192

The old woman saw a chance to get rid of the girl and replied, "Oh no, your majesty, I was telling my daughter that she works much too hard. She can spin three whole pounds of flax in a single day! The next day, she'll weave it into good linen cloth, and sew it all into shirts the following day!"

"That is amazing," he said. "Surely my mother, herself a great spinner, would be pleased with your daughter. Tell her to put her bonnet on and come with me. We might even make a fine princess of her, if she herself would like that."

The two women were thrown into confusion.
They had not imagined that the old woman's trick
would work so well. But the girl was soon ready
to be lifted up to ride behind the prince. The
mother received a bulging purse in exchange for
her daughter, and off they rode towards the palace.

It seemed that doing and saying little had served
the girl well, so when she got to the palace she
said few words, in the hope that she would not
look like a lazy idiot.

The queen showed the girl her room and the
work she was to do. "Here are three pounds of
good flax. I shall expect to see them turned into
thread by the end of the day."

The girl regretted that she had not listened to
her mother, and that she had not learned the craft
of spinning. She burst into tears and slept little
that night with worry and vexation.

When the morning came, the great wooden
spinning wheel was waiting for her, and the girl
started to spin. But her thread kept breaking, and
one moment it was thick, the next it was thin.

She burst into tears as the thread broke again.

Just then, a little old woman with big feet appeared in the room. "What is the matter, my fair maiden?" asked the woman.

"I have all this flax to spin, and whatever I do, the thread seems to break," said the girl.

"Invite me to your wedding and I will spin your thread for you," the woman offered.

"I will be glad for you to come to the wedding if you will do this work for me," said the girl. "I shall honor you for as long as I live."

195

"Very well. Stay in your room until evening, and tell the queen that her thread will be ready tomorrow," said the old woman.

The queen came, saw the beautiful thread, and told the girl to rest. "Tomorrow I shall bring you my fine wooden loom, and you can turn all this thread into cloth," she promised.

This made the girl even more frightened. She sat trembling, waiting for the loom. When the loom was brought, she sat at it and cried once more.

Suddenly, another old woman appeared in the room, a woman with great hips and a small voice, and she asked why the girl was crying.

"I have all this thread to weave, but I cannot work the loom," said the girl.

"Invite me to your wedding and I will spin your thread for you," the woman offered.

"I will be glad for you to come to the wedding if you will do this work for me," said the girl. "I shall honor you for as long as I live."

"Stay in your room until evening, and tell the queen that her cloth will be ready tomorrow."

The work was done and the queen was pleased. But this time, the girl found she had to sew the cloth into shirts for the prince. The girl was in deep despair, she had no skill with the needle. As she sat and cried a third old woman with a big red nose, appeared. The girl explained her plight.

"Invite me to your wedding and I will sew your shirts for you," the woman offered.

"I will be glad for you to come if you do this work for me," said the girl. "I shall honor you for as long as I live."

"Very well. Stay in your

room until evening, and tell the queen that the shirts will be ready tomorrow."

Again all the work was done, the queen was pleased, and the girl found that plans for the wedding were being made.

When the wedding came, it was the most lavish feast anyone could remember. The girl's old mother came, and the queen kept telling her how her daughter would enjoy herself spinning, weaving, and sewing after the honeymoon. As she talked about this, the footman approached the high table and announced another guest. "The princess's aunt, Old Woman Big-foot, has arrived." The girl blushed, but the prince was happy for her to come in.

When someone asked the old woman why her feet were so big, she explained that it was from standing all day working at the spinning wheel.

"My dear," said the prince. "I shall never let you

stand all day spinning."

Soon the second old woman arrived. When she was asked why her hips were so great, she said it came from sitting all day at the loom.

"My dear," said the prince. "I shall never let you sit all day weaving."

Finally the third old woman arrived and explained that her nose had grown big and red from bending down sewing, so that the blood ran always to her nose.

"Why, my dear," said the prince. "I shall never let you sit all day sewing."

So it came about that the lazy beauty never had to spin, or weave, or sew again, and she lived happily in her laziness at the prince's court.

Paddy O'Kelly and the Weasel

There was once a man called Paddy O'Kelly who lived in County Galway. Paddy had an old donkey to sell, so he got up early one morning for the journey to market. He hoped one day to buy a horse, though he knew he would not get enough money for the donkey to buy a fine steed that day.

Paddy went a few miles then it started to rain and he decided to shelter in a large house. No one was around, so he went into a room with a fire blazing in the grate. After a while a big weasel came into the room and put something yellow on the grate; then ran away. Then the weasel reappeared and put another yellow object on the grate. Paddy O'Kelly could see that they were gold coins.

When the weasel seemed to stop bringing the coins, Paddy got up, scooped them into his pocket, and went on his way. But he had not gone far when the weasel appeared, screeching and jumping up at him. She clung on until some passing men let loose their dog, which chased her away. In the end, she disappeared down a hole in the ground.

Paddy sold his donkey, and used some of the weasel's gold to buy himself a fine horse. He was returning home when the weasel popped up out of her hole and attacked the horse. It bolted, and nearly drowned in a nearby ditch, but two men helped him pull the beast out. Paddy was exhausted when he got home, so he tethered the horse in the cow shed and went straight to bed.

Next morning he saw the weasel run out of the cow shed. Paddy feared the worst, and when he got to the shed he found not only his horse but two cows and two calves dead on the floor.

Paddy gave chase with his dog. The weasel ran to a hovel by the side of the road, closely followed by the barking dog. When Paddy opened the door an old woman sat on a chair in the corner.

"Did you see a weasel coming in?" asked Paddy.

"I did not," said the old woman.

The dog leapt at the old woman, and she screeched with a noise like the weasel's cry. Paddy O'Kelly saw that woman and weasel were one and the same.

"Call off the dog and you'll be rich!" she shouted.

She explained that she had committed a great crime but she would be forgiven if Paddy took

twenty pounds to the church to pay for a hundred and sixty masses to be said for her. She told Paddy to dig beneath a bush in a nearby field, where there was a pot filled with gold. He could pay for the masses, and use what was left over to buy the big old house where first he saw the weasel.

"A big black dog might come out of the money pot," she warned. "He is a son of mine and will do you no harm. Soon I will die, and when I die, please do one thing more for me. Light a fire inside this hut and burn it and my body together."

Paddy found the pot of gold and as he lifted the lid from the pot, a black dog jumped out but Paddy remembered the warning. Paddy replaced his dead cows and horse, and bought a flock of sheep with the money. The priest arranged masses

to be said for the old woman. And he went to see
the man who owned the house where he had seen
the weasel. The owner warned Paddy that the
house was haunted, but Paddy insisted on buying
it, and stayed in the house all night, until a little
man appeared.

The little man's name was Donal. Donal played
the bagpipes and said that he was the old woman's

204

son, and that he would be a good friend, so long as Paddy told no one else who he was.

Then Donal said, "I am visiting the Fortress of the Fairies of Connacht. Will you come with me? You shall ride there on a horse provided by me."

At midnight, the two flew off on to of Donal's broomsticks. When they arrived, the fairy leader said, "Tonight we are going to visit the high king and queen of the fairies." They wanted Donal and Paddy to go with them, so off they all went.

When they arrived at the hill where the high king and queen of the fairies lived, the hillside opened up, and they walked inside. When all the fairies were assembled, the king explained why they were all gathered together. "Tonight we are to play a great hurling match against the fairies of Munster. The Munster fairy folk always have two mortals to help them, so we would like you to come with us."

When they arrived for the match, the fairies of

Munster were already there, so they began their game accompanied by bagpipe music.

When the Munster fairies were gaining the upper hand Paddy helped the little people of Connacht, by turning one of the opponents' human helpers on his back. Then the two sides started to fight, and before long the Connacht side were the winners. The Munster fairies turned themselves into flying beetles and ate up all the leaves from the trees and bushes until the countryside looked quite bare, then thousands of doves flew up and devoured the beetles.

Meanwhile the Connacht fairies returned to their

hill, and Paddy was given a purse of gold for his help. Donal took him back home, and he was back in his bed before his wife had noticed that he had gone.

Paddy had settled down to enjoy his riches, when Donal came to Paddy to tell him that his mother was dead. Paddy set fire to her hut with her body inside, as she had asked. Once it was burned to the ground, Donal gave Paddy another purse of gold, saying, "This purse will not be empty in your lifetime. I am going away, but whenever you take money from here, remember me and the weasel."

Then Donal was gone, and Paddy and his wife lived long and wealthy, and left much money and a farm to their children. They all did as Donal had asked, and whenever they spent some of his mother's gold, they spared a thought for him and the weasel who had led Paddy to his wealth, when he had gone to sell his old donkey long ago.

The Dream of Owen O'Mulready

Owen O'Mulready was a happy man. He lived with his wife Margaret in a pleasant house with a large garden. They had space to grow all the food they needed, and Owen's kind master paid him good wages. Owen had everything he wanted – except for one thing. Owen had never had a dream. He was fascinated by other people's dreams, and he very much wanted to have a dream of his own.

One day, Owen was digging potatoes when his master started to talk to him, as he often did. They talked about dreams, and Owen admitted he had never dreamt, and that he would love to have one.

"This is how to make yourself have a dream," said Owen's master. "Before bedtime tonight, clear the fire and make your bed in the fireplace. Sleep there tonight, and you will soon have a dream that you will remember for a long while, mark my words."

That evening Owen cleared the fire and made his bed in the hearth. When Margaret saw him doing this, she thought her husband was mad. But he explained, and she let him do what he wanted, for she knew how badly Owen wanted his dream.

So Owen got into his bed. He had not been asleep for long when there was a loud knock at the door. Owen opened it and a stranger was there. "I have a letter from the master which must be taken to America."

"You've arrived very late for such a message," replied Owen.

But he accepted the message, put on his boots, and went off, striding towards the west.

He met a young lad at the foot of a mountain. The boy seemed to recognize him, "Where are you going in the middle of the night?" asked the boy.

"I have a letter to take to America. Is this the way?"

"Yes it is. Keep going westwards. But how will you travel across the water?" asked the young lad.

"I will work that out in good time," said Owen. And on he went, until he came to the sea.

Owen found a crane standing by the shore.

"Good evening, Owen O'Mulready," said the crane, who, like the young lad, seemed to know Owen.

Owen explained his business and said that he was puzzled about how to get over the water.

"I will ferry you to the other side," said the crane.

"And what if you get tired before we arrive?" asked Owen.

The crane assured Owen that he would not get tired, and off they went, Owen on the crane's back.

They had not flown for long, when the crane started to tire. "Get off my back, Owen, for I am

beginning to tire," said the bird.

"But I'll drown in the water," said Owen.

Owen then saw some men threshing above his head. He shouted to one of the threshers: "Thresher, reach down your flail so that I can hold on to it and give the bird a rest."

The man held down his flail and Owen clung on. As soon as Owen had gone, the crane flew off with a mocking cry, leaving Owen hanging in the air.

"Bad luck to you!" Owen shouted at the bird as it vanished into the distance.

Owen's troubles were not over. The thresher shouted for his flail. "Let go of my flail, Owen O'Mulready. I cannot get on with my work." Owen said that he would fall into the sea, but the man still shouted for his flail, shaking it, as if trying to make Owen slip off into the water.

Suddenly Owen saw his chance. A ship had come over the horizon, and Owen shouted and waved with his free hand. Slowly the ship steered towards him but Owen thought he might not be able to hang on long enough.

"Are we under you yet?" shouted one of the sailors.

"Not quite," replied Owen. The ship came nearer, and the captain began to shout to Owen.

"Throw down one of your boots. If it lands on deck, we shall know we are under you."

Owen kicked one foot, and his boot fell towards the ship. But Owen did not see where it landed.

He was distracted by a terrible scream, and suddenly he heard his wife's voice shouting "Who is killing me? Owen, where can you be?"

"Is that you, Margaret?" asked Owen, not quite

sure where he was, or how she had got there.

"Of course it's me," replied Margaret.

Margaret lit a candle. The bed was covered in soot and she couldn't see her husband. He was up the chimney, clinging on with his finger tips. One of his boots had come off and had woken Margaret when it hit her on the head.

"So the master was right about your dream," said Margaret, smiling.

"Yes, he was right enough," said Owen. And Owen O'Mulready never wanted to have another dream again.

The King and the Laborer

A laborer was digging a drain when the king appeared and asked if he was busy in his work.

"I am, your majesty."

"Have you a daughter?"

"I have one daughter and she is twelve years old."

"I shall ask you one question," said the king.

"I am no good at questions," said the laborer.

"I shall ask anyway," replied the king. "How long will it take me to travel around the world? Have your answer ready by twelve o'clock tomorrow."

The laborer could think of no answer. When he got home, he told his daughter the king's question.

"Easy," she said. "If the king sits on the sun or the moon it will take him twenty-four hours."

At twelve o'clock the next day, the king arrived.

"Have you the answer to my question?"

"If you sit on the moon or the sun, your majesty, it will take twenty-four hours."

The king was impressed with the laborer's answer, but the man admitted that it was his daughter who told him.

"Well, here is another question for you," said the king. "What's the distance between the earth and the sky?"

The laborer asked his daughter, who told him what to do. "Take two pins and wait for the king. When he asks you what you are doing, tell him that will measure the distance from the earth to the sky, but that he must buy you a long enough line, so that you can make the measurement.

When the king arrived at twelve the next day, the man did as his daughter had suggested.

"A good answer," smiled the king, "but you did not think of it yourself." Again, the man admitted that his daughter had thought of the answer.

"I am impressed with your daughter," said the king. "She must come to my palace to work. If you allow it, I shall be a good friend to you."

So the laborer's daughter went to the royal palace and worked in the kitchens. She worked hard, the king was pleased with her work,

and the girl grew into a tall and beautiful young woman. But because she came from a poor family, the other servants teased her. When the king heard of this, he made her father a knight.

After a while the king and the girl were married. Afterwards, the king took his wife to one side and told her that he had something important to say.

"The queen must not speak against the king," he warned. "If you do, you must leave the palace."

"It would not be right for me to disagree with you," said the girl. "If you have to send me away, please grant me three armfuls of what I choose."

"I agree to that," said the king.

They soon had a son, which made them even happier, and the laborer still could not believe his luck in being made a knight. One day one of the king's tenants came to the king to complain to him. He had a mare that had foaled, but the foal always followed his neighbor's old white horse, and the man thought the neighbor wanted steal the foal. The neighbor insisted that the foal was his.

"This is how to solve the question," said the king. "Put the two horses and the foal by a gap in the wall. Lead out each horse and whichever horse it follows, her owner shall have the foal."

The king's order was carried out, and the foal followed the old white horse.

The queen heard what had happened and went to the wronged owner. "I must not speak against the king's judgement," she said. "But plant some boiled peas near where the king passes. When he asks you if you think they will grow, say: 'They're as likely to grow as the old white horse to give birth to a foal.'"

The king saw that he had been wronged. But he also guessed that such a clever ruse had begun with his wife. "Come here, wife," he said. "Leave the palace today, for you have judged against me."

"It is true that I did so, and I must go," said the queen. "Grant me the three armfuls I asked for."

The king was angry with her, but there was no going back on his word, so he indicated that she could take what she wanted. Then he was astonished when she carried him and his royal throne outside. "That is my first armful," she said. Next, she took the young prince and placed him in the king's lap. "That is my second." Finally, she gathered up an armful of all the royal charters and placed them with the prince. "And that is my third. I am happy to leave if these go with me."

The king saw that there was no parting with a woman of such wit. "Oh, dearest of women, stay with me!" he said. They went back into the palace together, and the king ordered that the foal should be returned to its rightful owner.

The Legend of Knockgrafton

By the Galtee mountains long ago lived a poor
basket-maker. He always wore a sprig of foxglove in
his hat, so everyone called him Lusmore, an old
Irish name for the foxglove. The most noticeable
thing about Lusmore was that he had a huge hump
on his back. This hump was so large that his head
pressed down and his chin rested on his chest.

When they first saw Lusmore, most people were
scared of him. But when they knew him, they
realized that he was one of the most charming and
helpful of people, in spite of such deformity.

One day, Lusmore was walking back home from a
nearby town. He found himself by the ancient
mound at Knockgrafton as it got dark. He still had
a way to travel, so decided to sit down beside the
mound and rest for a while.

220

As he sat down, Lusmore began to hear the most beautiful, unearthly music, with many voices singing different words, but blending in perfect harmony. Stranger still, the sound seemed to be coming from within the mound.

Lusmore was enchanted and eventually started to sing along with the music, blending his voice beautifully, making the song sound even better than before. Suddenly, Lusmore found himself picked up at lightning speed, and before he knew it he was inside the mound. Fairies danced around, obviously delighted that he had liked their singing and joined in. They danced around, in constant movement in time to the melodious song, and Lusmore smiled in amazement and enjoyment.

When the song was over, Lusmore watched the group of fairies talk among themselves, glancing at him and then going back to their conversation. He felt rather frightened, wondering what they would do to him. Then one fairy stepped towards him, chanting, "Lusmore, Lusmore, The hump that you bore, You shall have it no more, See it fall to the floor, Lusmore, Lusmore!".

Lusmore felt lighter, and found he could move more easily. Slowly, he lifted his head and found he could stand up straight, straighter than ever before. It was true! The hump was gone!

As he looked around him, noticing again the strange beauty of the fairies who had been so kind to him, Lusmore began to feel dizzy. A tiredness overtook him and he fell asleep among the fairies.

When Lusmore awoke, he found himself outside

the mound at Knockgrafton, in the morning sun.
He said his prayers, then gingerly felt his back.
There was still no hump, and Lusmore stood to
his full height. To his delight he noticed that the
fairies had dressed him in a smart new suit of
clothes. So off he went home, with a spring in
his step that he had never had before.

None of his neighbors recognized Lusmore.
Then they realized that he had lost his hump,
word spread quickly, and soon everyone was
talking about Lusmore's amazing good fortune.

One day, Lusmore was by his door working at a new basket, when an old woman appeared. "Good day," she said. "I am looking for Lusmore, who had his hump removed by the fairies. My best friend's son has such a hump, and if he could visit the fairies, perhaps he too could be cured."

The basket-maker told her that she had found Lusmore, and explained the story of how he had lost his hump. The old woman thanked Lusmore, and went back to tell her friend what her son, Jack Madden, should do to lose his hump.

Jack Madden set off for Knockgrafton, and sat down beside it. Soon he heard the sound of the fairies singing. Jack Madden was in a hurry to be rid of his hump, and joined in straightaway. He was a greedy fellow, who thought that if he sung louder, he might get two new suits of clothes instead of Lusmore's one. He bawled away as loudly as he could, almost shouting out the fairies in his eagerness to be heard.

Just as he expected, Jack Madden was taken inside the mound and surrounded by fairies.

The fairies were angry with Jack Madden and chanted: "Jack Madden, Jack Madden, You are such a bad'un, Your life we will sadden, Two humps for Jack Madden!"

A group of fairies took Lusmore's old hump and stuck it on Jack's back.

When Jack Madden's mother and her friend came to look for Jack, they found him with his two humps. They pulled at the new hump but they could not remove it. They went home cursing the fairies and anyone who dared to go and listen to fairy music. And poor Jack Madden had two humps for the rest of his life.

225

Fair, Brown, and Trembling

Long ago there lived King Hugh Curucha who
had three daughters. Fair and Brown were his
favorite daughters. They were given new dresses
and allowed to go to church every Sunday. But
Trembling, the most beautiful of the three, had to
stay at home to do the cooking and housework.
The other two forced Trembling to do this because
they were jealous of her beauty, and feared that she
might attract a husband before them.

After Trembling had been kept at home for seven
years, the Prince of Emania fell in love with Fair,
the eldest of the sisters. Fair and Brown went off to
church as usual, leaving Trembling to cook dinner.
As she worked, she talked to the old Henwife, who
kept the chickens on the royal farm. "Why haven't
you gone to church too?" asked the Henwife.

"I cannot go to church," replied Trembling. "All
my clothes are in tatters. I dare not go to church,

my sisters would beat me for leaving the house."

"What dress would you like?" asked the Henwife.

"I would like a dress as white as the snow, and a pair of bright green shoes," replied Trembling.

The Henwife put on her cloak, snipped a tiny piece of cloth from Trembling's dress, and asked for a beautiful white dress, and a pair of green shoes. They immediately appeared and Trembling put them on. Then the Henwife gave the girl a honey-bird to put on her shoulder, and led her to the door. There stood a fine white horse, with a saddle and bridle richly decorated with gold.

"Off you go to church," said the Henwife. "But be sure to stand just outside the church door. As soon as the people start to leave, be ready to ride off as quickly as you can." So Trembling rode to church, and did as the old woman had told her. Even so, many people caught a glimpse of her, and wondered who she was. At the end of Mass, several people ran out, but she turned her horse and galloped away.

Trembling was worried that no one had finished cooking dinner for her sisters. But the Henwife had cooked the meal, and Trembling put on her old dress as quickly as she could.

When Fair and Brown returned, they were full of talk about the mysterious lady in white. They demanded that their father buy them fine white dresses like the lady's, and next Sunday, they wore their new dresses to church.

Again, the Henwife appeared and asked Trembling if she wanted to go to church. The old woman produced a black satin dress, with red shoes for Trembling's feet. With the honey-bird on her shoulder, she rode on a black mare with a silver saddle, and stayed quietly by the door of the church.

The people in the church were even more amazed. Everyone wondered who she was, but Trembling rode away as soon as Mass was over.

Back home, Trembling removed her fine robe again, and put the finishing touches to the Henwife's meal. When Fair and Brown returned from church, they were full of talk about the fine lady and her black satin dress. "No one even noticed our fine dresses," complained Fair. "They were too busy admiring the lady by the church door and wondering who she might be.

Everyone was staring with their mouths open, and none of the men glanced at us!" Fair and Brown gave their father no peace until he bought them satin dresses and shoes, just like the one they had seen their sister wearing. Of course, Fair and Brown's dresses were not as elegant nor as finely made as Trembling's gown. They could not find one to match it anywhere in Ireland.

Off went Fair and Brown next Sunday in their new black dresses, and yet again the Henwife turned to Trembling and asked her what she wanted to wear to church.

"I would like a rose-red dress, a green cape, a hat and shoes of red, white, and green."

The Henwife once more did her magic, and Trembling was dressed in her chosen clothes, and mounted on a mare with diamond-shaped spots of white, blue, and gold over her body. The honey-bird began to sing as Trembling rode off to church, to wait outside the door.

News had spread all over Ireland about the lady who stood outside the church every Sunday. Amongst the lords and princes waiting to see her was the Prince of Emania. Once he had seen Trembling, he forgot all about her elder sister, and vowed to catch the lady before she could ride away. At the end of Mass, the prince sprinted out of church. He was just able to grab hold of one of her shoes, before she galloped away into the distance.

The Prince of Emania vowed to search the length and breadth of Ireland until he found the woman whose foot would fit the shoe. The other princes joined in, as they too were curious. They searched in every town and village until they came to the

house of Fair, Brown, and Trembling. Both Fair and Brown tried the shoe, but it was too small for them. The prince asked if there was any other woman in the house.

"Only a serving-girl we keep to clean the house," said Fair. But the prince insisted that every woman should try on the shoe.

The prince was thrilled when the shoe fitted exactly. Trembling ran very quickly to the Henwife's house, who helped Trembling on with her white dress; then she returned home to show everyone that she was truly the mysterious lady.

She did the same thing with the other dresses, amazing her sisters more and more each time. The princes were just as surprised, and before she had put on the third dress, they were all challenging the Prince of Emania to fight for her hand.

The Prince of Emania fought bravely, defeating the Prince of Lochlin, who fought him for nine hours, the Prince of Spain, who fought for eight hours, and the Prince of Greece, who fought for seven hours. And at the end no one would fight the Prince of Emania, for they knew he would be the winner. So the Prince of Emania married Trembling, and the celebrations lasted for a year and a day.

Fair was still very jealous of her sister. One day, she called on her sister, and the two walked by the coast. When they came to the sea, Fair waited until there was no-one to see her, then pushed Trembling into the water. It seemed as if Trembling would drown, but a great whale came and swallowed her. Fair returned to the prince, put on her sister's clothes and pretended to be Trembling.

Although the two were as alike as could be, the Prince was not fooled by her trick.

Fair thought that no one had seen what she did, but a young cow-boy had watched the two sisters from a nearby field. The next day when he was in the field he saw the whale swim by and throw Trembling on the sand. She told the cow-boy to tell her husband what had happened and that if he did not shoot the whale, she would stay under the whale's spell and never be able to go home."

The cow-boy ran to tell the Prince what had

happened, but Fair gave him a potion to drink which made him forgetful, and he said nothing about what he had seen. The same thing happened the next day. On the third day, when the cow-boy was by the sea and saw Trembling cast out yet again, the girl guessed what had happened and spoke to him, saying "Do not let her give you any drink when you go home. She is using a potion to make you forget what has happened."

And so finally the prince was brought news of his wife. He ran to the shore, loaded his gun, and shot the whale, releasing Trembling from the creature's spell. From then on the cow-boy lived in the Prince's household, and when he came of age, he married Trembling's daughter. They all lived happily, for many years, until the Prince and Trembling died, contented, of old age.

The Haughty Princess

There was once a king who had a very beautiful daughter and many dukes, earls, princes, and even kings came to ask for her hand in marriage. But the princess was proud and haughty and would have none of them. She would find fault with each suitor, and send him off with a rude remark.

She said to a plump suitor, "I shall not marry you, Beer Belly." To a pale faced suitor she said, "I shall not marry you, Death-Mask." And to a third suitor who was tall and thin she said, "I shall not marry you, Ramrod." A prince with a red complexion was told, "I shall not marry you, Beetroot." And so it went on, until every unmarried duke, earl, prince, and even king, had been rejected, and her father thought she would never find a man she liked.

Then a prince arrived who was so handsome and polite, that she found it hard to find a fault with him. But the princess's pride won, and she looked at the curling hairs under his chin and said, a little reluctantly, "I shall not marry you, Whiskers".

The poor king finally lost his temper, "I'm sick of your rudeness. I shall give you to the first beggar who calls at our door for alms, and good riddance to you!"

Soon a poor beggar knocked at the door. His clothes were in tatters, his hair dirty, and his beard long and straggling. Sure enough, the king married his daughter to the bearded beggar. She cried and and tried to run away, but there was nothing for it.

237

The beggar led his bride into a wood. He told her that the wood and the land around belonged to the king she had called Whiskers. The princess was even sadder that she had rejected the handsome king, and hung her head in shame when she saw the poor, tumble-down shack where the beggar lived. The place was dirty and untidy, and no fire burned in the grate. The princess put on a plain dress, helped her husband make the fire, clean the place, and prepare a meal.

The beggar gathered some twigs of willow, and after their meal, the two sat together making baskets. But the twigs bruised the princess's fingers, and she cried out with the pain. The beggar was not a cruel man, and so he gave her some cloth and thread, and set her to sewing. But although the princess tried hard, the needle made her fingers bleed, and again tears came to her eyes. So the

beggar bought a basket of cheap
earthenware pots and sent her
to market to sell them.

The princess did well at
market on the first day,
and made a profit. But the
next morning, a drunken
huntsman rode through the
market place, and his mount
kicked its way through all the
princess's pots. She went home in tears.

The beggar spoke to the cook at the palace of
King Whiskers, and persuaded her to give his wife
a job as a kitchen maid. The princess worked hard,
and the cook gave her leftovers to take home for
her husband. The princess liked the cook, and got
on quite well in the kitchen, but she was still sorry
she had rejected King Whiskers.

A while later, the palace suddenly got busier, King
Whiskers was getting married. "Who is going to
marry the king?" asked the princess. But no one
knew who the bride was going to be.

The princess and the cook decided to go and see what was going on in the great hall, they hoped to catch a glimpse of the mysterious bride. They opened the door quietly and peeped in.

King Whiskers was in the room, and strode over when he saw the door open. "Spying on the king? You must pay for your nosiness by dancing a jig with me." The king took her hand, led her into the room, and all the musicians began to play. But as they whirled around, puddings and portions of meat began to fly out of her pockets,

240

and everyone in the room roared with laughter. The princess began to run to the door, but the king caught her and took her to one side.

"Do you not realize who I am?" he asked her, smiling kindly. "I am King Whiskers, and your husband the beggar, *and* the drunken huntsman who broke your pots in the market place. Your father knew who I was, and we arranged all this to rid you of your pride."

The princess was so confused she did not know what to say. All sorts of emotions welled up inside her, but the strongest of all these feelings was love for her husband, King Whiskers.

The palace maids helped her to put on a fine dress fit for a queen. She went back to her husband, and none of the guests realized that the new queen was the poor kitchen maid who had danced a jig with the king.

The Man Who Never Knew Fear

• • • ● • • •

There were once two brothers, called Lawrence and Carrol. Lawrence was known as the bravest boy in the village. Carrol, on the other hand, was fearful of the least thing, and would not go out at night.

When their mother died, they had to decide who would watch her grave. In those days it was the tradition that when a person had died, their relatives would take it in turns to stand guard over the grave, to protect it from robbers.

Carrol, who did not want to watch his mother's grave at night, made a bet with his brother. "You say that nothing makes you afraid, but I bet you will not watch our mother's tomb tonight."

Lawrence replied, "I have the courage to stay there all night." He put on his sword and marched boldly to the graveyard, where he sat down on a gravestone next to his mother's tomb.

At first, all went well, but then he became drowsy. As he was dropping off to sleep Lawrence saw an awesome sight. A huge black head with no body was floating towards him. Lawrence drew his sword ready to strike if the thing came any closer. But it did not, and Lawrence stayed, looking straight at the head, until dawn.

When he got home, Lawrence told Carrol what he had seen. "Were you afraid?" asked Carrol.

"Of course I wasn't," replied Lawrence. "You know very well that nothing in the world will frighten me."

243

"You will not go again," taunted Carrol. "I would, but I have missed a night's sleep. You go tonight, and I will watch the third night." said Lawrence.

But Carrol would not go, so Lawrence slept and then went to the graveyard at dusk. A huge monster appeared scratching about near his mother's grave. Lawrence chopped the monster up with his sword. The graveyard was peaceful until daybreak.

Carrol was waiting for his brother to come home. "Did the great head come again?" he asked.

"No, but a monster came and tried to dig up Mother's body," said Lawrence.

At the final night of watching, a creature appeared with a man's head and long fangs. Lawrence reached for his sword, but the ghost began to speak: "Do not strike. You have protected your mother's grave, you are the bravest man in Ireland. Great wealth awaits one as brave as you. Go and seek it."

The next day Lawrence took the fifty pounds he had won from his brother in the bet, and set out to seek his riches. On his way he met a baker, and told

him the story of his adventures. "I'll bet you fifty pounds you'll be scared by the graveyard here," said the baker. "Go tonight, and fetch the goblet on the altar." The baker knew the church was haunted, and that no one ever came out of the building alive. That night, Lawrence strode up to the church door, hitting it firmly with his sword. An enormous black ram, with horns as long and sharp as scythes appeared. Lawrence struck the creature, and it fled, leaving blood all around the church doorway. Then Lawrence took the goblet, and went to the baker.

The baker was astounded that Lawrence had returned in one piece, and they went to see the priest to tell him the news. The priest was so pleased that he paid Lawrence still more money.

Lawrence had traveled through lonely countryside when he came to a valley crowded with people watching two men playing a ball game, but the crowd seemed to be frightened. Suddenly, one of the players hurled the ball towards him. Lawrence saw that it was the head of a man and as Lawrence caught it, it screeched, "Are you not afraid?"

"No I am not!" said Lawrence, and the head, and the crowd of people, vanished from sight.

When Lawrence reached a town he was weary and needed lodgings. A young man he told about his quest pointed to a large house across the road. "Stay the night in there and you will find something to put fear in you. If you can stand it, I will give you fifty pounds more."

Lawrence made his lodgings inside the cold, dark cellar. The first night, a bull and a stallion fought in the room with a fearful neighing and bellowing. Two great black rams fought in the room the next night, screeching and howling loud enough to wake the whole town. Still Lawrence did not feel fear.

On the third night an old man's ghost appeared.
"You are the bravest man in Ireland," he said. "Do
one thing for me and I will give you great riches."
The old man told Lawrence how he had wronged
a woman called Mary Kerrigan and he wanted
Lawrence to beg her forgiveness. Then he could
buy the house and marry the old man's daughter.

Lawrence went to Mary Kerrigan and won her
forgiveness. He bought the house, and all the land
around it, and married the old man's daughter.
They lived happily in the house, and the ghosts
never returned.

The Missing Kettle

There was a woman who lived on the island of
Sanntraigh, who only had a kettle to hang over the
fire to boil her water and cook her food. Every day
one of the fairy folk would come to take the kettle.
She would slip into the house quietly without
saying a word, and grab hold of the kettle handle.

When this happened, the kettle handle clanked
and the woman looked up and recited this rhyme:

> *A smith is able to make*
> *Cold iron hot with coal.*
> *The due of a kettle is bones,*
> *And to bring it back again whole.*

Then the fairy would fly off with the kettle and
bring it back later, filled with meat and bones.

One day the woman had to go on the ferry across
to the mainland. She asked her husband to say the
rhyme when the fairy came for the kettle. Her
husband agreed and went back to his work.

The fairy arrived and the husband saw her come to the door. When he saw the fairy he started to feel afraid because he had had no contact with the little people. "If I lock the cottage door," he reasoned to himself, "she will go away and leave the kettle, and it will be just as if she had never come." So the he locked the door and did not open it when the fairy tried to come in.

But the fairy flew up to the hole in the roof where the smoke from the fire escaped, and made the kettle jump right up and out of the hole.

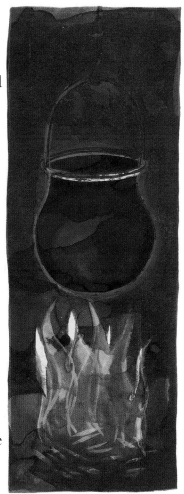

The fairy made off with the kettle in a trice, and when his wife returned that evening, there was no kettle to be seen.

"Where is my kettle?" asked the woman.

"I've done nothing with it," said the husband. "I took fright when the fairy came and closed the door to her, she took the kettle through the roof, and now it is gone."

"You pathetic wretch! Can't you even mind the kettle when I go out for the day?"

Off went the woman to the knoll where the fairies lived, to see if she could get the kettle.

It was quite dark when she arrived. The hillside opened to her and when she went in she could see an old fairy sitting in the corner so she thought that the others must be out at their nightly mischief. She found her kettle, and noticed that it contained the remains of the little people's food.

As she ran down the lane with the kettle she heard the sound of dogs chasing her. Thinking quickly, she took out some of the food from the kettle, threw it to the dogs, and hurried on.

This slowed the dogs down, and when they began to catch her up again, she threw down more food until she reached her house, ran in and closed the door, hoping they would not come inside.

Every day after that the woman watched for the fairy coming to take her kettle. But the little creature never came again.

Jamie Freel

Jamie Freel's mother was a widow, with little spare money. But Jamie was a very hard-working lad, so they usually had enough to eat. Near where Jamie and his mother lived was an old ruined castle. People said this was where the little people lived. Jamie had seen them at Halloween when all the windows of the old ruin lit up, and he could hear their music inside the thick stone walls.

The more he listened to the fairy revels, the more fascinated Jamie became. When Halloween came round, he decided to go to the castle, peer through the window, and see what was going on.

So Jamie called to his mother, "I'm just away up to the castle, to see what is going on there tonight."

"Oh Jamie! Don't risk your skin going there," said his mother. "I might lose you to the little people."

"Have no fear, mother," he called out as he left.

The little people noticed him looking through the

castle windows and called out his name. "Welcome, Jamie Freel, welcome! We're off to Dublin tonight to steal a young lady. Will you come with us?"

Jamie liked the sound of this, and was soon flying through the air at alarming speed with the fairies. They landed in a grand square in Dublin and before long the fairies had kidnapped a young woman and carried her all the way back home.

Jamie was getting anxious for the feelings of the young lady, so when they were near home, he asked if he could have a turn to carry the girl.

When they arrived home he quickly put her down at his own door.

The fairies grew spiteful. "Is that all the thanks we get for taking you to Dublin?" they screeched. And they tried turning the girl into all sorts of different shapes – a black dog, a bar of iron, a wool sack, but they failed. In the end one of the little folk threw something at the girl. "There's for your treachery," screamed the fairy. "Now she will neither speak nor hear." Then they flew off leaving Jamie and his mother staring at the poor girl.

At first, Jamie's mother could little think how they would look after a Dublin girl who could neither speak nor hear. But the girl helped the widow with the cooking and housework. She even helped outside, feeding the pig and the fowls, while Jamie worked away mending his fishing nets.

The three settled down together, but sometimes the girl looked sad and Jamie and his mother guessed that she must be thinking of her home.

When Halloween came again, Jamie decided he would go and see the fairies once more. He crept up to a window, taking care not to be seen this time. Soon he heard the fairies talking about what had happened a year before. The fairy who had made the girl deaf and dumb said: "Little does Jamie Freel know that a few drops of this liquid would cure her."

Jamie burst into the castle and stole the liquid while the little people were welcoming him. Then he ran home and gave the girl the liquid before anyone could stop him.

Jamie and the girl decided that now she could talk again, they would go to Dublin to find her parents. But when they knocked at the door, no one recognized her. Her parents insisted that their only daughter had been buried over a year ago. She showed them her ring but they accused her of being stealing the ring and pretending to be their daughter.

Jamie and the girl realized that they would have to tell the people the story of the fairies. Then the old man and woman saw that they had been deceived and that this indeed was their daughter. They showered the girl and Jamie with kisses.

When the time came for Jamie to return home, the girl wanted to go too, for the pair had become inseparable. The girl's parents realized that the two should be married, and sent for Jamie's mother to come to Dublin for the grand ceremony. Afterwards they were all happy, and Jamie felt that all his hard work had been richly rewarded.